TWISTED HAIR

Myth and legend interweave with history and prophesy when the Twisted Hair tells the stories of the Cherokee people

O'Siyo
Holly McClure
Wado

Holly McClure

NEW VOYAGES PUBLISHING
ST. SIMONS ISLAND, GA.

Twisted Hair. Copyright © 2002 by Holly McClure

All rights reserved. No part of this publication may be reproduced, stored in any retrieval system or transmitted in any form or by any means, electronic, mechanical, photocopying, recording or otherwise, without the prior written permission of the publisher.

Published by
New Voyages Publishing
210 North Harrington Rd.
Suite 201
St. Simons Island, Ga. 31522

International Standard Book Number [ISBN]
0-9718746-0-3

Printed in the United States of America by
RJ Communications LLC
51 East 42nd Street
Suite 1202
New York, NY 10017

Design and layout
Jonathan Gullery
HSA design
4 West 43rd street
New York, NY

First Printing

This book is dedicated to the Eastern Band Cherokee people
And to all the story tellers who remembered the stories and
passed them down to us through the generations. In my
childhood they still spoke of the days of the removal as if it
happened yesterday, for the pain had not left them.
They taught me to look for Awi Usdi, the Yunwi Tsundi
and the immortal Nunne'hi when I walked in the forests
of Graham County, for they still believed. They watched events
unfold, and recognized the fulfillment of prophesy. They warned
of things to come, and now I observe as they come to pass.
Their voices are silent, but their wisdom still lives, if we
are wise enough to hear.
      Thank you for allowing a little mixed blood girl
to listen.

INTRODUCTION

Who is Twisted Hair?

In Native American tradition, stories and storytellers were honored. It is said that a traveler called, the Twisted Hair, journeyed across the land through all tribes and nations. He was welcomed even among enemies of his own people because he was a teller of stories. His badge of office was a hair style. Long hair, twisted into ropes and bound with beaded thongs, marked him as an honored guest among all tribes.

Twisted Hair was not one man, but many. His descendants still carry on his work. The stories in this book are inspired by them and their stories. The history and prophesies are told as I remember hearing them. Only the way they are told is original to me.

The Council House Mound still stands, not far from where I grew up. I heard that the town that used to be there was taken into the mountain to protect it from the changes to come with the arrival of the white man. There, the elders still live to hold the wisdom for their children's children, and wise people still go there to seek it. I can think of no better place for the Twisted Hair to reside, waiting until the time when his people have need of him, and are ready to listen. Then, he will walk among us once more.

Twisted Hair brings the story of the people.

CHAPTER 1
TWISTED HAIR

He comes

From the seacoast he walks inland. Past the great mound cities on the waterways. Through smaller towns and villages in the hills and plains. Shouts of welcome lift his spirit and the time he spends with old friends eases the fear he cannot conceal. He tells them stories that were old in the days of the ancestors and says they must remember, for they teach the sacred ways that give them strength. In each village, he implores the people to keep his stories in their hearts and teach them to the children. When he takes up his staff and walks away, he leaves the taste of his fear with them. They talk of the shortness of his stay and wonder what has brought such great sadness to his eyes.

He does not tell then that his fear and sorrow spring from a new story he carries with him and cannot tell? He holds it in his heart and waits, traveling always toward the hills, to a place known as *The Mountains Covered with Smoke,* or in the tongue of the people, *Sha-cona-gee.* The untold story is a burden heavier than the pack he carries on his back. He hurries on, not lingering in any town long enough to rest for there is no time. The end of his journey is near.

The path is wider now and well trod. The man's steps are silenced by a thick carpet of pine needles. His back stoops beneath his burden but he is not slowed. Beside him on either side, walk the dogs, each with his own burden. Their noses lift to sniff the air.

He comes!

Behind him walks a young boy, his load now heavier for he carries the pack his dog carried when the day began. The dog limps, his left front paw held to his chest. The trail has been hard for them all. The man sniffs the air, his nostrils almost as keen as those of the three dogs. The breeze carries odors of cooking fires and curing hides. The unmistakable scent of people who live the way human beings live everywhere he travels, close together in their little towns and villages. They are drawn to each other like the buffalo is drawn to the herd.

Only he lives alone. . . He and the boy.

He comes!

It's almost in sight now. He remembers. Just beyond the rise he will see down into the valley, to the thick wall of logs that surrounds the lodges. Already he can see thin wisps of smoke drifting high above the trees in the distance. Before the sun sets he will be in the town of healers. It is a place where wise ones keep the sacred ways and offer comfort to troubled spirits. He has need of their wisdom.

He adjusts his heavy pack, his broad back straight in spite of the load, and then strides ahead. The journey has been long and hard but this sacred village hidden deep within the mountains is the only place he can tell his story. The wise ones will know what to do. The boy stands tall as he sees the man has done, his own sturdy young body shaking off the fatigue of the long walk. It is time. They will soon be seen.

The man holds his head high and breathes deeply of the clear mountain air. He begins to sing.

Two small boys who are gathering firewood with their mothers are the first to see them.

"HE COMES!"

Their shouts ring out and others run to join them. First come the children. Then the women drop their bundles of fire wood and run out to meet the man, the boy, and their three dogs.

"HE COMES!"

They shout it to those who might not have heard, and the people run to meet them. It is a joyful crowd that follows the man and the boy. They sing a welcoming song until they reach the palisade that surrounds the village. It is three times as tall as the tallest man and made of sharpened tree trunks stood on end. At the entrance, the people stand aside to let the man enter first.

The entrance is narrow and straight, leaving room for only one to enter at a time. Single file they walk until the walls angle and narrow. A large animal, like a bear, would be unable to get through, and human enemies knew better than to try.

A few more steps and they are inside the village. A tall man, straight and strong in spite of his years, and an old woman, greet the man and boy and bid them lay down their burdens. Their presence loosens the knot in the man's belly but his fear finds its way into their hearts. One look into his eyes and they know he brings a new story this time. They will not welcome it, but it is a story they must hear.

Young men take the heavy packs. The man and the boy stretch, grateful to finally be free of the weight they carry as they walk the land. The boy is quickly surrounded by the young people of the village, curious, and a little awed that he travels with the man. He soon drifts away with them, his limping dog at his side.

The old woman leads the way. The man walks behind her, led by the tall man who is the Uku, or peace, chief of the town. He knows the chief's authority is no greater than the old woman's for she is the Ghigham, or Beloved Woman, a title she earned by years of wisdom, strength and courage. The Uku bears his authority with the humility of the holy man he is. One with power such as his does not need to show a proud face.

The man can feel the eyes of many people upon him. It is meant to be so. The richness of his clothing is worthy of notice. His strong body and handsome face is to be admired. Long hair, twisted into thick ropes and bound with beaded thongs, hangs almost to his waist. It is different from the men in this village or any other. The difference sets him apart. This too is meant to be for it gives him his name and marks him as one who can walk in safety among all the people of the land. Even the sworn enemies of his own people honor the Twisted Hair.

He lifts his staff in greeting. Adorned with the carved likenesses of the clan totems of his people, it has been spoken of for generations and is as much a part of his legend as the strange way he wears his hair. Those nearest him strain for a closer look. They will want to describe it to their own children and grandchildren.

The Ghigham halts before a door and calls out. In answer to her call, the hide covering is drawn aside by a slender dark hand. A young woman steps out into the evening shadows and stands silently before him, her eyes modestly lowered. The men who carry his packs place them inside her home. It is here he will lodge until he leaves this village.

The young woman's husband has been away for four seasons. There are some who say he will not return. Her eyes say she still hopes. The Ghigham knows one cannot live on hope.

With her eyes still lowered, the young woman holds aside her door and welcomes the man into her home. He is pleased with his lodging, and soothed by her gentle smile.

The men who carry his packs talk among themselves about the weight of their burdens and speculate about the riches they contain. Perhaps they hold red jasper from the coast or turquoise from the west. Tomorrow they will see. Trading will not take place before then. Now they must see to their own trade goods. He will want healing herbs to take to the lowland towns and rattles made from deer hooves. There is time to get them ready.

The man waits in the lodge of the sad eyed woman. Soon, the Uku will come for him. It is he who will bring sage and cedar to cleanse and purify him then take him to the cold clear river beyond the walls. There he will plunge seven times beneath the rushing water to wash away impurity and restore harmony. This time, the boy will come with him. He has reached an age to take on some of the duties of the Twisted Hair. His spirit must be made ready.

Night falls, and the fire before the council house is fed. As it leaps into the growing darkness, the people gather in the shadows cast by its dancing flames. The man has eaten well, the best to be had in the whole town, and is rested from his journey. Drums sound and the voices of singers call to any who have not already come. A few rise to dance. The women hold their heads high, their eyes always looking forward, and glide in a slow, sedate motion. Always toward the center, they dance, their feet never losing contact with the earth for in this way they draw strength from the Mother. The men whirl and leap, lifting hearts and celebrating the strength of their people. The dancing and singing don't last long. That is not the purpose of this gathering.

He is come. Twisted Hair brings the stories of their people.

Silence descends as he rises to his feet. First, the stories for the children. Their solemn black eyes shine in the firelight. Even the smallest is still and quiet. . . waiting.

"Long time ago" he begins. His voice is soft but in the silence it carries to the farthest edges of the fire's shadows. "Earth was covered with water."

All but the youngest already recognize the story.

"Ahhh," the old ones sigh, and find places to sit in comfort on their blankets, to listen once again. Never would they grow tired of hearing how the beloved mountains and valleys of their home came to be.

"Galun-lati was crowded. There was no place to be alone. The people there looked down at Earth and waited for the water that covered it to dry up. A long time passed and still water covered Earth as far as they could see. If there was a dry place where some of the people of Galun-lati could live, it could not be seen from the above world. Someone must go and search for it.

A small grey dove looked down upon the water. She was not the strongest of the people of Galun-lati but she had courage. "I will go," she said, and on her soft wings she soared off the walls of the above world and down to Earth below. Even though she flew the circle of the world, she found no dry place to land.

On she flew, seeing only water until her wings grew tired and her people feared she would be too weak to come home. She listened to their calls and struggled back to the walls of Galun-lati.

"There is no place for us. Earth is covered by water." She said.

As time passed, Galun-lati grew even more crowded, for there everything grows fast and many children are born. The people looked down and hoped for a dry place on Earth.

Raven flew to the walls. "I am bigger and can fly farther than Dove," he said. "I will go search for land." He flew from Galun-lati and soared around the circle of the Earth. Water still covered the land. On and on he searched and still no dry land appeared. Even Raven's strong wings grew tired in time, and he had no choice but to return home before he fell into the water and perished.

The people feared there would never be a dry place on Earth for them to live. They waited, looking down and still saw nothing but water.

At last, the oldest of them all came to the wall. Grandfather Buzzard lifted his great black wings and swooped down to the world below. They feared for his safety and called him to come back home. It was not good for a beloved elder to go into danger. Their cries followed him as he soared away into the distance."

Twisted Hair's arms are lifted and the fire casts his shadow behind him. His robe silhouetted by the flames, looks like great black wings. The children will remember that they saw the grandfather of the buzzards this night.

"The people watched from the walls of Galun-lati as Grandfather Buzzard circled the Earth, searching for a place for them to live.

When Moon rose in the sky she saw that he still circled. . . searching. Sun Father watched him as he flew through the day.

Grandfather Buzzard grew tired but he would not give up. The people in Galun-lati called to him, "come back, Grandfather." They saw that his wings drooped till they reached beneath the water into the thick mud below. With failing strength he lifted them until again they drooped. Each time he brought his wings from the depths of the water, mud stuck to his feathers.

He flew on. As the people watched, they saw the mud that stuck to his feathers, piled up to form mountains. The beat of his wings dried the water, and valleys appeared. At last his strength deserted him. Thinking he had failed his people, he gave up his struggles. Instead of falling into the water as he expected, he landed on a dry mountain peak. There he folded his great wings and rested.

In Galun-lati the people looked down on the valleys and mountains of Sha-cona-gee and rejoiced to see the land that would become the home of the Ani-yun-Wiya."

The great black wings swoop upward once, then away as Twisted Hair folds his arms and sits on his blanket. He takes the pipe offered him.

For a while there is silence; then comes the gentle voice of an old one, a grandchild on her lap. "And his grandchildren still circle as he once did over the land. In this they honor him."

Others like her speak to the little ones. All lift their eyes to the dark shape of the mountains that encircle their valley and whisper prayers of thanks. A drum sounds and a lone singer lifts his voice in a song to Sha-cona-gee, The *Mountains Covered with Smoke.*

Then again, the silence, as the Ani-Yun-Wiya think of the legend of the great buzzard.

The Uku speaks in his quiet way, "He did not have the beauty of the eagle or the sweet song of other birds, but he was one to be honored, for he too was part of the balance and harmony of all life."

The boy who traveled with Twisted Hair sits a little apart, listening to each story and song, attending every comment made by the people, then holds them in his heart. He has already gained a store of wisdom far greater than most men.

Twisted Hair draws from the pipe, reverently watching the thin smoke drift upward. A young man adds wood to the fire. A fresh cedar branch spreads incense as it burns. Again the storyteller rises.

"It is not only Grandfather Buzzard who has made Earth a good place for us. Others of the animal people give of themselves to make our lives pleasing. They have done so from the beginning."

The elders nod in agreement as he continues.

"Long time ago when the first people were on Earth, the four leggeds, the water people, the feathered people, all looked at themselves and said "this is good." They spoke of their rich thick fur, their shiny scales or soft feathers. They gave thanks to Unehlanuhe, the creator, for sharp horns or antlers, long claws or hooves. For their sharp teeth and for the way they could run fast or swim in the river or fly into the sky.

The animals grew strong and were many on the Earth. They were happy, until they began to look at the poor two legged people, the human beings. The two leggeds were naked. They had neither fur nor scales nor feathers. They had no horns or antlers, no sharp hooves or teeth or claws. They were not strong like Bear or fast like Rabbit. They were weak and cold and often hungry. Their children didn't grow strong and their numbers were few.

Now, the animals were wise and knew that every one was needed. They understood that all things were created in balance, and if the humans died, their place in the Earth would be empty. They feared the time would come when there would be no more two legged people. Coming together in council, they talked about what could be done to save the Human Beings.

Awi Usdi, The little white deer, chief of all the deer people spoke to the animals. "If the humans are to live they must have food that will make them strong, and shelter so their children can grow. We must give ourselves to the humans so they can live."

The animals agreed. They would allow the humans to take some of them for food, but in return, the human beings must honor the animals and remember the prayers and ceremonies that would send them to Galun-lati to wait the time for their return to the forest.

Awi Usdi walked among the humans while they slept and told them what the animals had decided. When the humans awoke, each talked about the dream they had of a little white deer who spoke to them.

From that day, the humans began to hunt the animals as they were told in the dream, but they remembered the prayers and ceremonies the little white deer had given them, and took only what was needed. The human beings grew strong and their numbers increased. They were well fed and the furs of the animals made warm robes that kept out the cold. Animal skins covered their lodges, and they were warm and dry even in the cold times. Children grew up and filled the villages.

For many generations of the humans, all was well. But a time came when no one could remember the dream of the little white deer, or that the animals had given themselves to save the humans. They only remembered that they were great hunters, and the pleasure they took in hunting. Many animals were killed who were not needed by the humans. The hunters no longer honored the animals nor remembered the ceremonies and prayers they had been taught by Awi Usdi. Worst of all, the humans had invented a new weapon which no animal could outrun. It reached out into the forest and brought the animals down. With his bow and arrow a hunter could kill many animals.

The animals were afraid. If something was not done to stop them, the humans would kill all the animals and the balance they had sacrificed themselves to maintain would be lost. The animals decided to try to fight back, but before an animal could get near enough to fight with a hunter, an arrow would fly from the bow and the animal would die.

The animals knew that the only way to fight humans was with their own weapons. Bear made a fine bow, as good as the ones the humans had, but when he tried to shoot it, his long sharp claws became entangled in the bow string and cut it in two.

Without his claws, Bear believed he could use the bow. He bit them off and tried again. Sure enough, he could shoot as well as the humans. It seemed that the answer had been found until Bear started to climb a tree to reach a bee hive and feed on the honey. Without his claws he could not climb the tree. He tried to tear open an old tree trunk to feed on the grubs inside but could not, because his claws were gone.

No. Bears could not take off their claws to use the bow. Again the animals called to Awi Usdi. The little deer returned to the forest and spoke to the animals. "The humans began to hunt because I came to them in a dream and offered our flesh and skins to save them. They have dishonored our sacrifice. Tonight when they sleep, I will speak to them again."

That night as the humans slept, Awi Usdi walked among them once more. He scolded the sleeping people for the way they dishonored the animals who had given their own bodies to save the humans. He reminded them of their promise to take only what was needed, and of how they had broken their word. They had wasted the animals and forgotten to offer prayers and songs to send them back to the above world. He promised that hunters who took only what they needed and remembered the proper ceremonies, would remain strong. But all who betrayed the gift of the animal people would suffer.

When the human beings awoke in the morning, they spoke of dreams of the little white deer. Some heeded his words and were sorry for the way they had treated the animals. Always, they honored the animals with the prayers and ceremonies the little deer had given. Those who did this stayed strong and healthy.

Other hunters said, "I too dreamed of the little white deer," then they forgot his words and went on with their ways, wastefully killing the animals and forgetting to honor them as Awi Usdi had said. For them it was as the little deer promised. They suffered. Their bones ached. Their joints became swollen and stiff. Their hands twisted and knotted into claws that could not hold a bow.

It is so to this day. The hunter who honors the animals and thanks them for their meat, taking only what is needed and leaving the rest to live, stays strong and healthy. The hunter, who does not, suffers."

A man near the fire pulled his blanket closer, hiding his gnarled fingers between its folds. He hung his head for he knew the young boys looked his way.

He remembered the days when he had been a great hunter and the pleasure he took in the kill. If his crooked hands could hold a bow he would still bring home more meat than his family could eat.

    The storyteller sat and let silence seal his words in their hearts. They thought of Awi Usdi and the other animals who lived in their stories. From the edge of the crowd, a hunter's voice lifted in a song he always sang as he made his way through the thickets and forests. The song kept him safe. When the song was over, a voice came from the silence. "Tell us of Yellow Rattler's song."

    A look of infinite sadness settled over the hunter's features as he told of the gift of this sacred song. "Long time ago, when the animals still spoke with human beings, a chief of our people left his family to go hunt. He knew his wife and sons were safe because there was peace with all the created beings after many generations of war. A hard law kept the peace; the law of retribution. The law said that any harm you did to another, could be avenged in like measure by his people.

    The chief's wife was busy grinding corn for bread while she watched her children. Her little one crawled into the grass and then began to cry. She ran to see what had frightened him. There at his feet, coiled as if to strike, was a great red rattle snake.

    As is the way of a mother, all thoughts left her mind except the safety of her child. The grinding stone was still in her hand. Her fear made her throw harder than she intended for instead of frightening away the snake, the heavy stone crushed his head.

Her regret could not restore Red Rattler's life. She sent her older son to take the dead snake to a place beside a trail his people used, so they would find him.

Her husband knew nothing of this as he traveled toward a valley where game was plentiful. As he neared the valley, he heard many mournful voices lifted in a death song. He listened, long enough to know they mourned the death of a great chief. Climbing to the top of the ridge, he looked down to see a gathering of all the snake tribes, weeping around the body of Red Rattler. His heart was touched by their grief. He went to them and asked, "Who is so beloved that his death could cause so much sorrow?"

Yellow Rattler, the war chief of the snakes answered him. "Our great peace chief, Red Rattler was killed today in your town."

The man was overcome with grief and remorse and began to weep. He stayed with the snake people, grieving with them, making offerings and honoring Red Rattler. He sang the snake chief's death song with his people, and then sat outside their council house while Yellow Rattler and his warriors spoke of retribution for Red Rattler's death.

Yellow Rattler came to him and said. "By the law of retribution, the death of our chief must be avenged. The council says that all who live in your town must die before your people and mine can live in peace again. Today, I will lead my warriors against your people."

The man cried out to the council saying, "I am a chief of my people, just as Red Rattler was your chief. Take my life and your chief is avenged. Spare the life of the people in my town, for surely only one is guilty of slaying your chief."

The council replied that he, of all his people, was most innocent. His death would do nothing to avenge Red Rattler. The warriors made ready to attack the town.

The man followed Yellow Rattler, pleading with him for the life of his people. "One of my people is guilty of this great wrong," he said. "If you will not accept my life as retribution for the life of Red Rattler, then take the life of his murderer and let the innocent ones in my town live."

Yellow Rattler said, "My brother. If we agree to do this, will you bring the murderer to me?"

The man's heart was heavy when he agreed to do as Yellow Rattler asked. He would betray one in his town to spare the life of the rest. There was nothing more he could do.

In great sadness, the two warriors set out to the man's town, Yellow Rattler and the man. As they traveled, they talked of the burden of their duties and shed many tears.

In the town, they passed the lodges of the man's clan and others of his people. At each door he thought of the ones who lived there, hoping it was not this one he must send to Yellow Rattler.

When the only lodge left was his own, grief made him falter. Yellow Rattler said, "It must be done, my brother, or my people will come tomorrow and no one will be spared."
The man could only nod in agreement.

"Send your wife to the spring for fresh water," Yellow Rattler said. "I will be there."

The woman welcomed her husband and put food before him. "I would like fresh cold water from the spring," he said. She took the water pot and went for fresh water. He sat with his children, waiting.

"Father," his son said. "I heard my mother cry out."

"Be still, my son," the man said.

They waited, and the woman did not come with the water. Instead, Yellow Rattler came to the house and coiled in the doorway. "It is done," he said. The price is paid. Your people are safe. My people grieve with you as you have grieved with us. Never again will you or your children's children need to fear the snake people. I give you a song. Sing it when you travel in our land and my people will honor it and leave you in safety."

To this day, we sing Yellow Rattler's song, and live as brothers with his people."

The man softly sang the song that protected him and his family from snake bite, while some whispered of the great price the man's ancestor had paid to save his people and keep peace between the snakes and the human beings.

The stories, the songs, and the silence continued as Full Moon climbed into the sky. Most of the stories, the people knew for they were of the kind told around the fire. There were others that would not be repeated here. They would be told when only a few were there to hear. The ones who knew these stories kept them sacred, telling them only to others who were worthy and would preserve them for future generations. These were the stories that kept the people strong. If they were lost, the power that preserved the Ani'yun Wiya would be lost with them.

Other stories, the man brought with him from his travels. Stories told at firesides like this one by people far away. One he told was new to them. It was a story of creation, but not like the ones they knew. The creator in this story was a woman who wove all things into existence. She spun a web, and in the web were all the people, animals and the green growing things. The woman was all powerful and greater in size than Earth Mother herself. She had no form but when she chose to take a shape, she appeared as a spider. The people who told her story called her Grandmother Spider.

All were quiet as they thought about this strange new story. The Uku raised his head and spoke. The people listened closely to what he had to say for they knew he was wise and his medicine strong.

"This is good," he said. "She has all power and can take any form she wishes, but she honors one who is among the smallest and most humble of all creatures when she takes the form of the spider. This we must remember. Even the smallest is worthy of honor for she is a part of the balance."

The Ghigham spoke quietly, "Even with her great power she takes a humble form for herself. She knows the danger of too much pride." This was a lesson the Ghigham, herself, must remember.

The Uku nodded. "Our people have not always remembered how the overbearing pride of a few can bring trouble to all. The way my grandfather told it to me was. . . Long before our time, lived a family called the Ani'-Kut ani. They knew all the stories and had strong medicine. Their house was a seven sided lodge upon a great mound of earth. The mound was filled with the bones of their dead. They claimed to draw power from the dead bones. For a few generations the Ani'-Kut ani cared for the people, keeping the raven mockers from the sick so they couldn't take and eat their hearts and steal their last days of life, to add to their own. Our people feared the Ani'-Kut ani but their power kept us safe from sickness and harm.

As their power increased, so did their pride. They took what they wanted without regard for the needs of the people. They no longer cared for the weak or protected the sick. If they wanted a woman they paid no heed that she had already taken a husband, or that she did not consent. They took her and used her without respect. They claimed the right to do whatever they wanted because they were born Ani'-Kut ani. They said they were descended from the immortals and could speak with the spirits. Our ancestors lived in fear of them.

The time came when a young man with a good name went away to hunt. When he returned, his wife was gone, taken away by the Ani'-Kut ani. His grief and anger made him brave. The people had only waited for one with the courage to lead them against the evil people. Following the brave young man up the mound they slew all who were of the blood of the Ani'-Kut ani. Never, since that time, has any one family held a place of power over our people. Sacred knowledge is given only to those chosen by The Great One, and the creator of all does not care about what family or clan they were born to."

A respectful silence held until the Uku was seated and the pipe was at his lips. They watched as he drew deeply one time, and then passed it on, his eyes on the thin curl of smoke drifting up into the darkness. He was one whom The Great One had chosen. They trusted him with their sick for they knew the raven mockers feared him.

Twisted Hair thought about what he had heard. The story was new to him. He must remember it. He had seen cities built around earth mounds with chiefs who held power by virtue of their blood. Some he visited were as corrupt as the Ani'-Kut ani, but their people did nothing to protest. It was good to be here away from the weakness and decay he sensed in some of the lowland towns. These mountain people had strength, and here in this sacred town, there was wisdom and healing. He had done the right thing to bring his story here. They would know what to do. He looked at the Uku beside him. Yes, they would know what to do, when it was time.

He took the pipe one more time, and then stood. "It is good you have a trusted one to keep away evil," he said in an ominous voice. "In a village not far from here the raven mockers took many an elder, or those who were sick or hurt. They were seen, flying through the air, their arms outstretched like wings with fiery sparks trailing behind them. A sound like a strong wind was heard and in the wind, the cry of the raven. When the sound is heard it is known that a life will soon go out. When no one in a town has medicine strong enough to keep him away, the raven mocker goes unseen into the house and takes the heart of the sick one. He leaves no scar. Whatever time was left to the victim is owned by the raven mocker, as soon as he eats the heart.

I was in a town when a young man went out hunting. The deer were scarce and darkness would fall soon. He must return home empty handed, but he was tired, and still a long way from home. Since he knew of a house nearby where a man and a woman lived alone, he decided to go there to sleep warm for the night and hunt again in the morning.

When he reached their house, no one was there. He called out to them but heard no answer. An asi stood just outside the house. Just as in his village, the little sweat lodge was used for sleeping on cold nights. A small fire could keep it warm. He went to it and stooped down to look in. Coals still smoldered in the fire, but no one slept inside. His bones were tired and the warm asi was a good place to rest so he crawled to the far side and curled up against the wall.

Just as he was falling asleep, he heard the sound of a strong wind outside, and in the wind, the cry of a raven. The wind died as suddenly as it came. He opened his eyes to see the man bend over to crawl into the asi. He listened as the man stirred the coals and added wood to the fire. The smell of meat cooking filled the little round sweat house. Careful not to make a sound, the hunter looked up and saw what looked like a heart roasting on a stick over the fire.

Again the sound of a strong wind and a raven's cry, then the woman entered the asi and sat across from the man. The hunter was brave, but even so he trembled with fear as he listened to the woman and man talk.

"How many did you get?" the woman asked.

"Only one," the man answered, "and I need it all. How many did you get?"

The woman's voice was sad when she spoke. "In the town where I went, a warrior was hurt, but the Uku there had such power that I could not even enter. I am hungry, and I'm beginning to feel old."

Then the hunter knew for sure he was in the asi of raven mockers, the most feared of all the skin changers. And worse, one of them was very hungry. His fear made the hunter breath heavy. The woman heard him. She took a stick from the fire and shined the flame to the place where he lay. The hunter made his heavy breaths sound like snores and pretended to be asleep. When the light reached him he rose up and rubbed his eyes to make them think he had been asleep all the time. As he hurried out, he thanked them for the warmth of their asi in which to take his rest, and then ran all the way back to his village. When he arrived, he told us what he had seen and heard."

Twisted Hair paused to let them think about the danger the young man was in, and then continued. "We followed him back the house of the raven mockers. Sun was coming over the mountain by the time we got there. We went to their door and called out. There was no answer, but we could see inside. They lay as if asleep. The women gathered cedar branches and placed them around the house, for it is known that evil beings like raven mockers cannot cross cedar.

We did not know what to do then, for there were no wise people with us and no warriors who knew how to slay the skin changers. We were all afraid for many in the town had died before their time. We talked of how the raven mockers had taken them and stolen their last days of life.

While we talked of these things, someone, we never knew who, set fire to the cedar branches. Never have I seen a fire burn so fast. In no time, there was nothing left of the house but cinders and ashes. I watched as they prodded among the ashes and gathered up a pile of blackened bones. That's all that was left of that man and woman. The raven mockers were dead."

Twisted Hair raised his eyes to the darkened sky and stood still and silent, listening to the people whisper about how good it was the skin changers were dead and could not harm them.

He gave them a moment to feel safe, and then they took note of how he watched the sky as if searching for danger sweeping down from the night. When the silence was so deep his softest voice could be heard he said, "They say the man and woman had children."

A shudder ran through the crowd as they too looked at the sky. How lucky they were to have an Uku with medicine so strong he could keep skin changers away, and young men and women who learned from him. They spoke of how people came from many tribes to listen to the wisdom of the Uku and the other holy people who kept their village strong. Many thought about gifts they would make to the old holy man. He would have plenty of tobacco, meat, corn, and anything else he needed before tomorrow ended, but the night was still young and there were other stories to tell.

A young warrior told of how his grandfather had seen Uktena, the great serpent. He said it coiled around a mountain with his monstrous head resting on the peak. The crystal 'Ulunsu-ti' crowned his head and glowed blood red in the sun. He told of the brave young warrior who many years ago had slain the serpent and claimed the Ulunsu-ti and the power it held. There was no greater power than the Ulunsu-ti. The only way to obtain it was to kill the serpent and take the talisman from his head

    The Uku stood once more. His words were heeded by all, for his was the knowledge and power that healed their sickness and kept away harm. "Do not speak lightly of Uktena or the Ulunsu-ti." There was warning in his voice. "There was a time when the serpent took many lives of the Ani-yun-Wiya. When his life begins, he is no bigger than a grub and eats small things. As long as he lives, he grows. When he is of a size, he eats all the animals and people he can find, and then moves where he can find more. No one is safe when Uktena is in this world.

    I do not doubt that he was seen by this man's grandfather. The serpent lived near here, on the mountain where nothing grows. His blood and poison are what made the mountain bare. In another town, there lived a proud man who boasted of his strong medicine and his might as a warrior. Men who had lost many of their people to Uktena, heard him. They would make use of the great wonders the foolish man could work. The men captured him and sent him to kill the serpent.

    He traveled the land, seeking the place where Uktena lay in hiding, for he was foolish enough to think the serpent was small enough to hide or had need to. In one town the people led him to a cave and told him the serpent was there. He killed the monster inside, but when he went to claim the Ulunsu'ti from its head, he found only a great toad lying dead in the cave.

When he came to the mountain where Uktena lived, he saw the great body coiled round the mountain all the way to the top. Only when he looked at the size of the monster's head and sharp fangs, did he become humble enough to call upon the Creator for help.

Unehlanuhe heard his call and showed him the only way the life of Uktena could be taken. The foolish man listened and did as he was told. It was not through his own knowledge that he killed the serpent.

He was too ashamed of his boastful ways to return to his own people who knew him as a proud and arrogant conjuror. When he claimed the Ulunsu-ti from Uktena's head, he made an oath to use it and the power it gave him for the good of the people who took him to live among them. He still keeps his vow, but he grows old and soon will walk over to the other world. The one who holds the Ulunsu'ti after him must be strong."

When the Uku was quiet, the warrior spoke again. "The Uktena is dead and we no longer need fear him."

The Uku said, "Uktena cannot die. He is one who lives forever. He lives within the Ulunsu'ti until he is freed to take form, then once again he will grow until he is as fearful as the great serpent. Someday another will need to kill him before he eats everyone. There will be many who try. Greed for the Ulunsu-ti will make them brave, but it will take more than greed and courage to slay the great serpent."

For a while the people talked about the danger of Uktena and the many stories they had heard of him. Some claimed he had been seen again. The Uku listened with lowered eyes and thought of the bundle secreted away in his lodge, guarded by a trusted warrior. His sleep would be forever haunted by the monster and the battle he fought, but it was worth it. His people were safe and well, and good things had come to the village. Yes, when rightly used, the Ulunsu-ti was good medicine. With the help of the Nunne'hi, the Uktena would remain imprisoned inside the crystal where he could do no harm.

Another told of seeing the Dakwa swimming under his canoe, and said he feared the great fish would devour him as it had so many others. Some told of the times when human beings and animals could speak to each other. Great warriors and hunters were remembered and their deeds brought to mind.

An old woman told of a boy she had known when she herself was just a child. "Many times I helped his sister look for him when he wandered away," she said. "His sister scolded him and told him to stay with the other boys, but he would forget. One day he walked away and we could not find him. When he came home he looked no different than when he left. The clothes he wore were the same. Nothing about him had changed, but his sister and I were different. Since he was lost, we had grown old enough to have children and grandchildren.

He cried for his mother but she had walked over to the other world. The people who were children with him were now old, and he was still a boy. When we asked him where he had been for so long, he said he had only been gone three days. He followed the music he said, and the sound of dancing, until he found where it was coming from. He hid for a time and watched the dancers. They were little, no taller than his knee and beautiful to look at. They found him when the grass he was hiding in tickled his nose and made him sneeze. He was afraid, but they were kind and took him to their village. There he stayed and was well fed and cared for until they sent him home.

He took us to the place where they lived. He said their village was very beautiful with ripe corn fields and great chestnut trees. We found nothing in that place but a hedge of laurel around a bare hillside. He cried for a long time. He cried for his mother and grandmother and all his friends who were now men and women, not children as he had left them. Everyone had left him behind while he was gone. Time was different in the land of the little people called Yunwi Tsunsdi, for that is where the boy had been."

She sat solemn and quiet while the children thought about her story. There was no need for mothers and fathers to admonish their children not to wander away alone. They didn't want to be taken away, to come home and find everything changed, their parents old or dead and their friends all grown up while they were still children. Some mothers were seen to smile at each other over the heads of their little ones.

Someone asked a mother to tell about the Nunne'hi woman who had helped her find her own lost child. The people smiled, for no one feared the immortal Nunne'hi. "Was she beautiful, and strong?" they asked.

"All Nunne'hi are strong and beautiful," she answered. "It is good they have a town near our own. They have always helped us when we needed them."

An old man told again of how they had taken him to their town and cared for him after an injury that would have killed him if not for their help. "A river clear as the air ran through the town," he said. "The fruit trees were filled with ripe fruit and blossoms at the same time. Corn fields were full of ripe corn and roasting ears, both on the same stalk. Never have I seen a more beautiful town or kinder people. When I was healed, they took me beyond a grove of blossoming peach trees with ripe fruit hanging thick on the branches, and pointed me to the path home. Don't look back, they said, but when I stepped beyond the grove of trees and into the snow, I longed to see the sunshine again. I looked back, but saw nothing there but a bare hillside."

"It is always that way with the Nunne'hi," the Ghigham said. They and their lands cannot be seen unless they wish it."

Late into the night the stories continued. Some of the children fell asleep and were carried to the warm asi beside the house of their family and put to rest for the night. The boy stayed at the storyteller's side long after the rest of the young ones had gone.

At last, only the Uku, the Ghigham and the other wise elders were left sitting by the dying fire with Twisted Hair and the boy. Now, the story that weighed down his spirit and troubled his dreams could be told. His face paled in the moonlight and his voice trembled. "A new evil has come to our land." he said. "He wears pale eyes and a white skin and holds in his hand the end of the world. Where he walks he brings death. His weapons kill with the sound of thunder. When he goes he leaves bodies of our dead and sickness that takes the ones he left alive. I went to a town where he had been. I had gone there before when many strong people reaped a rich harvest. The store houses were full and the people strong and whole. When I returned only an old man still lived among burned lodges and graves. He told of the evil ones. He said they were the *Turtle People* named in prophesies, for they were men who walked like turtles. From head to toe they wore shining shells that protected them from harm. I have traveled to many towns and found them in ruins with only a few of the people left alive. They told of strangers who came, bringing death. It is as the prophets foretold. The *Turtle People* have come to bring the end of the world."

  He watched the fear he had carried in his own heart settle, over the people of the healing village and had no story that would offer hope. "It is a long way from their ships to the land of Sha-cona-gee," he said. "For now, we are safe here in the Mountains Covered with Smoke."

  The rising sun found the elders still sitting by the smoldering embers with Twisted Hair and the boy. Any hope that their wisdom would hold an answer had vanished in the night. Even the Uku had no medicine to turn aside an evil such as this.

  Days and nights passed in the healing village. The knot of fear Twisted Hair had brought with him eased while he rested in the lodge of the gentle woman. It pleased him to see that sadness no longer clouded her eyes and she smiled when he sat at her fire. He had no wish to leave her house, yet he knew the time would come. His work in the lands beyond the village waited.

The war chief took warriors to scout the trails for signs of the stranger's approach and returned to say he had seen no sign of them. Messengers went to other villages to ask for news and returned with nothing but rumors of unease.

A morning came when the Uku and the Ghigham entered the young woman's lodge. The council had spoken and Twisted Hair's time of rest and peace had come to an end. He must go take his story to the wise people of other towns and prepare them for the coming of the strangers. At the time of harvest he would return and bring word of what he had learned.

Sadness returned to the young woman's eyes. "His place is here," she said to the Ghigham. "He is a holy man and keeper of knowledge of our sacred ways."

The Uku agreed with her. "The Twisted Hair is a holy man, but his work is beyond these walls and among our people wherever he finds them. Generations yet unborn will look to him for the knowledge concealed in his stories. In the days of the children's children, they will still look to him, for his wisdom will be needed even more in times to come." He embraced Twisted Hair and said. "Your road will be long, my son and rest will not come soon." Infinite sorrow aged his features as he looked beyond the distant hills, as if he saw the future of his people. He and the Ghigham said farewell to the storyteller and left him to prepare for his journey.

The woman's smile left her face when he walked away. His own sadness weighed heavy as he and the boy took up their packs. With the three dogs, they left the only place in the land he had ever called home. He promised to return at harvest time but her face mirrored his own fear that he would never see her or the healing village again.

They spoke of him and the boy often after he left. They war chief and his warriors kept watch for the strangers and prepared for the time they would appear, but the village nestled among the protection of the Mountains Covered with Smoke, remained as it had for generations. People came from many tribes to learn from the wise ones and to find healing for body or spirit. Winter came and went. The people kept the festivals and cycles of seasons just as their ancestors had in generations past. Hunting was good and the people were content. Talk of the Turtle People died down and was almost forgotten, but not by the war chief and his warriors. Not by the Ghigham, the Uku and the wisest of the elders. Fear of what the strangers would bring to their world was with them day and night.

"In their hands they hold the end of the world," the Uku said.

The Ghigham nodded and said, "Yes, the end of our world."

CHAPTER 2

VOICES IN THE WIND

*C*orn was ripe in the husk and the weather hot and still on a late summer day. The Ghigham had almost filled her basket with the many-colored grain when the wind picked up. It was cool on her face. She stopped her harvesting and faced into the breeze. Suddenly, a strange look came to her face and she stood still, listening. Within the breeze, whispered voices spoke and their words brought fear to her heart. She dropped the harvest basket and began to run, past the other women, up the hill to the council house. The Uku was already there. As soon as she saw his face she knew he too had heard.

"Do you hear what they say?" she cried. "It is as Twisted Hair said. The strangers will come. Our sacred ways, our songs and stories, all that keeps us strong and in harmony, will be lost. They say everything will change. That many of our people will die and many who live will become like the strangers and forget our ways. They say our people will be driven away, far from the sacred lands of Sha-cona-gee. But what they ask us to do. To be sealed inside this mountain. To no longer be mortal but to live as the invisible Nunne'hi. Is it the right thing?"

There were tears in the Uku's eyes. For many generations the Ani'yun Wiya and many other tribes had come from far and wide to this town, to learn the sacred ways that kept them strong. Now, the

Nunne'hi spoke in the wind, to warn of the end of the town and the wisdom it held.

"We will wait," he said. "We will see if others hear the voices. Then we will take it before the council. It will be decided by all the people, whether we will do as the voices ask."

The Ghigham nodded and went back to her harvest.

The next day a hunter returned from the forest with a deer across his shoulder. He was happy. His wife would be pleased with the meat he brought her. The wind from the mountains cooled his face. In the wind a voice spoke. He stopped to listen, and then hurried home. His wife greeted him, hardly noticing the deer he brought.

"Did you hear?" she asked.

"I heard," he answered. "Your mother will help you with the meat. I will go to the council house."

Others were already there to meet him, the war chief, the peace chief, warriors, mothers and fathers. They had all heard the voices and needed guidance and reassurance from the Ghigham and the Uku.

The peace chief had lived a long and happy life in the town of healers. He didn't want to see changes come. Their village had been smiled on by Unehlanuhe even more than other villages of the Ani'yun Wiya. Life was good here and had been for many generations. The healing village was needed by all the people who came to learn or find harmony. Sacred ways that had been forgotten in other villages were remembered here, for the sake of all the people, now and in generations to come. The peace chief understood why the voices were heard here and not elsewhere.

"If we do as they say, we can stay as we are forever. We can keep the wisdom and ways of our people when they are forgotten by the rest who stay outside."

The War Chief spoke. "But to be a captive inside the mountain, never to leave our own village. To stay safely here while our people on the outside are in danger. I am not willing."

The warriors who sat with him let it be known they agreed. They did not fear the strangers. When they came, they would die. The warriors were sure. It was always so when an enemy came against them.

The Ghigham lifted her hand for silence and spoke. "The voices that speak in the wind gave us seven days to make up our minds. They first spoke yesterday, then again today. Two days are gone. Five are left." She turned to the war chief. "Send your warriors through the village to gather all the people who are still outside. When all have spoken, we will decide."

The people came to sit in council. Some said they would refuse the voices and stay outside. Others, though afraid, said they were willing to enter the council house on the seventh day as the voices had said and wait to be sealed against the world.

On the morning of the seventh day, only one young woman remained outside the council house, her eyes on the path that led from the hill. It was not time for Twisted Hair to return but her heart still hoped. The Ghigham went to her side. "He has work he must do," she said. In silent sorrow, the young woman dried her tears and went inside to wait with the rest for the Ghigham to speak. Her words would tell them what their lives would be. They listened as her voice came softly across the fire.

"The strength and hope of our people lies in the knowledge of our sacred ways. If this is lost, it is the end of hope for us, in our time and in the time of our children's children. For the sake of those yet unborn, we will do as the voices ask. With us will live the wisdom for all who come to seek it. We are chosen to hold it for them. For this purpose, we must be sealed apart from the world. Within this mountain we will live as the invisible, immortal Nunne'hi. . .forever."

Stillness settled over the people as they waited for the moment when their days in the world would come to an end. Thoughts of Sha-cona-gee, the beloved Smoky Mountains beyond the village walls, filled them with longing but they would obey. They walked the way of harmony in this and all things.

The war chief broke the silence as he leapt to his feet with a loud cry. "No! I will not hide in the land of the Nunne'hi while our people perish." Brave warriors echoed his cry. With no time for farewells they followed him as he rushed from the council house. The ancient town of their ancestors remained long enough for one brief look, then a great wind swept down from the mountain. Cold, as the heart of winter, it caught and held them like twigs in a whirlpool, then as suddenly as it came, died away.

The warmth of late summer once more touched the land but nothing else was the same. The town of the healers was gone. The protecting palisade no longer encircled the place their home had been. Where once there were houses and gardens, the warriors saw nothing but a barren, rocky mountain side.

They looked for the council house but it and all their people were gone. In its place, a stone mound in the form of the seven sided council house jutted from the mountain side.

***

Inside the mound, the people of the town opened the council house door and walked outside. The warriors who had just departed were not there, but the village looked the same as it had before. The corn awaited harvest. Dogs napped in the sun and the town stood as it had for generations. Encircling mountains rose beyond the wall, marking the edge of their world. Nothing beyond it existed for them.

It was enough.

***

On the path leading to the town, a man and boy walked with their dogs. Tired from a journey made in haste, they were almost home. The voices who had spoken to Twisted Hair in the wind said he was needed there. They topped the hill but no shouts of welcome reached their ears and no one ran to meet them. Searching the valley for the smoke that should have been drifting upward from the cooking fires, they saw nothing. Not even the smell of a town lingered in the clear air.

They ran down the hill and along the trail but where the village had stood, they found no sign of its existence. Only the war chief and his warriors remained of their people, and they were leaving. "We are not needed here," the war chief told them." Our people are gone from this world. The Nunne'hi took them into the mountain. We go to defend our land against the strangers who have brought the end of our world." He gestured toward the mound. "The ones you seek are inside. You are too late." He left them and led the warriors away.

    Twisted Hair stood before the mound, searching for an entrance but saw only a seamless rock face. Inside was the Uku, the Ghigham and all the wise elders. The woman who waited for him, waited inside, alone. He and the boy remained behind in a world where they had no home. He called the woman's name, knowing she would not answer. Not even a bird's song or a cricket's call broke the silence. This had become a place of the Nunne'hi, where no bird, animal or creeping thing ventured.

    Why did they call him back and then close the way to him? He climbed to the top of the mound, hoping the Nunne'hi would speak again in the wind but no voice came in the breeze. In despair he sat on the cold stone, remembering the wisdom of the Ghigham, the power and kindness of the Uku and the gentleness of the people. Remembering the young woman who waited. They were lost to him, for those sealed inside could never return to the mortal world. He understood why they had chosen to leave the mortal world. Inside the mound, the knowledge they held could be preserved for generations yet to come, but what of the wisdom he alone carried. He knew many things that even the wisest of the elders had not learned. Would the sacred wisdom in his stories be forgotten when he and the boy no longer walked the land?

A drumbeat reached his ears, so faint he thought it only a memory. As he listened it became clear. Voices from deep within the mound rose in song. They sang a story of an ageless Twisted Hair who lived inside the town of the healers. While generations passed in the world outside, his people would remember him and wait for the time when he would walk among them again. In the days of the children's children, the promise of his return would give them hope. When they faced their greatest peril, he would come with forgotten wisdom and awaken memories of sacred ways.

The song brought understanding. He would join the people in the hidden village to take his rightful place with the wisdom keepers. When his stories were needed to restore harmony to the descendants of the Ani'yun Wiya, he would journey to the land of mortals. His work was with them when the time came. Until then, he was home.

The boy waited before what was once the doorway to the council house. Twisted Hair called to him then took his hand and helped him climb atop the mound. The whisper of muted voices through the stone brought a look of wonder to the boy's face. He heard the song of the Twisted Hair who would remain in the timeless land and return to the mortal world in time of need. He learned a story of holy people who preserved the sacred knowledge for all who could find their way to the mound to listen.

The last song was of a boy who would take up the staff of the Twisted Hair and walk the land alone, for he must tell the story of the sacred hidden town.

The boy understood. A new story had been given and he must take it to the people. In dark days to come, they would hear of the wisdom keepers and find hope. A few would travel there and listen. The knowledge held here would never be lost to the world. The world outside was changing and he was afraid, but a great duty was his and he must not fail. This was his purpose from the day he followed the Twisted Hair from the lodge of his people. Now, he was the storyteller. His work was before him. They listened until the song ended and the Nunne'hi came for Twisted Hair. The time had come to part.

Twisted Hair embraced the and boy gave him the great totem staff. "Take it, for you are the storyteller now," he said. "You are ready. Go, and let our people know that here, the knowledge lives. When you are old and tired, come here to rest."

The boy stood tall and tried to hide his trembling. He could not speak, even to say goodbye. The Nunne'hi guided them to the doorway then turned to the boy. He would not come inside with the Twisted Hair for he had many things to do before they met again. The Nunne'hi placed his hand on the boy's head. Some of his fear left him but even the touch of the Immortal could not ease his sorrow. He had known no father but Twisted Hair and parting brought an ache to his heart. A long time would pass before they met again, for the gift, or the curse, of the Nunne'hi was the extension of his mortal life. Generations would be born and die by the time he left the world.

Twisted Hair embraced the boy one last time, and then walked with the Nunne'hi into the stone. For a moment, the boy caught a glimpse of the village inside, and then only the cold stone remained. He was outside, alone in the world and too young to hide his tears. They flowed freely as he twisted strands of his long hair into ropes, the way he had watched the man do for most of his life. When it was done, he took up the great totem staff of the Twisted Hair. It was awkward in his hands but he would grow to hold it as easily as the one who carried it before. Now he must dry his eyes and begin a journey filled with dangers no Twisted Hair had faced before.

    He turned from the mound and walked into the world alone to tell his story.

CHAPTER 3

A STORY OF HOPE

Into a changing world the boy traveled with his story of unchanging wisdom. Where the people had lost hope, he told them of a wise man who would come in times of trouble, telling stories and teaching the sacred ways. Everywhere he went he prepared the way for the return of Twisted Hair. When they asked when this would be, he looked into the distance and said softly, "I do not know." In his heart, he hoped it would be soon but this was not to be.

Years passed, and still he walked the land alone, remembering a mound shaped like a seven sided counsel house, and the wisdom that lived there. The knowledge he held seemed small compared to that of the wise ones in the hidden village, but he had learned much traveling with Twisted Hair. Some, he would tell to all who gathered to hear his stories. Other things he would only speak of when most had left the fire for the night and only the wisest remained. They were the ones who would understand when he told them of a place where they could learn from the wisdom keepers in the hidden village.

Generations came and went. The boy became a man, and then grew old. The Nunne'hi's gift of long life, allowed him to see many changes and grieve the death of many friends. He lost count of the seasons that passed, and still he journeyed, tired and alone, telling his story of the Ghigham, the Uku, and the healing village that disappeared into a myth long ago. Even when the story was well known by all, he told it.

The healing village and the wise ones who waited there would not be forgotten. In his stories, they lived and were always wise.

In every town, a few would linger late into the night and ask, "How can I find the Council House Mound?" He would tell them of Sha-cona-gee, the Mountains Covered with Smoke. A few would journey to that place and some would find the mound. All who came in a sacred manner to wait and listen would hear the song of the wisdom keepers. In the stillness of a hidden place in Sha-cona-gee, they sang for the sake of the children's children. For that purpose the Nunne'hi had spared them. Knowing this made his long journey worthwhile.

Throughout the land, he traveled while the years passed. While the touch of the Nunne'hi made his life longer than other men, age had marked him on the evening he entered the silent town in the lowlands. He was tired and hoped for a winter's rest with people who had sheltered him in other cold seasons. This time, old friends did not come to meet him on the path. No cries of greeting reached his ears. Even when he walked among the lodges, no one called his name. This was not the first town where he had been greeted only by empty lodges and silence but the grief never lessened.

Cold winds blew across the hills. Soon snow would fall. The chill cut him to the quick and his body ached with fatigue. It was good there was still shelter to be found in the town, for he could travel no more. He placed his pack and the totem staff of the Twisted Hair inside an empty lodge, and brought wood to the asi beside it for a fire. When the fire had burned down to coals and the stones in the fire pit glowed red, he closed the opening and poured a pot of water on the heated stones. Steam filled the asi. He sat naked while hot steam pulled the ache and fatigue from his body and eased the grief in his heart.

When morning came, traces of a dream stayed in his thoughts. It seemed the Twisted Hair with whom he had traveled as a young boy, spoke to him, reminding him of the days of his childhood when he had left his people to follow the storyteller. It awoke the memory of loneliness when his mother and father died and of the Twisted Hair who helped him forget his sadness.

On a hill near the village, he greeted the sun and offered prayers to Creator. In the stillness, he heard the soft cry of a child, quickly muffled by his mother's hand. He followed the sound to a crevice under the hill. There, a woman cowered in fear, clutching her son to her breast. She had hidden with him, listening to the cries of her people as the strangers rounded them up to be taken away as slaves. Some, like her, had fled and some had died trying to escape.

He knew they could not stay in the empty village. The strangers were nearby and there were still goods for them to plunder in abandoned lodges.

The horse he rode had belonged to one of the strangers. A warrior had won it in battle and gifted it to him. It made his journey easier and helped him save the woman and her son from the fate suffered by most of the people in her town. They left the same day, traveling North up the course of the creek.

In a few days they came to a village too small to be noticed by the strangers. The people of the town welcomed them and cared for the woman through the winter. When they gathered around the fire on cold evenings to listen to his stories, the child sat close by the storyteller's side. With his eyes closed, he sat so still he seemed to sleep, but he was listening. The storyteller noticed and knew the boy heard each word and held it in his heart, for he had done the same many years ago as he sat beside the Twisted Hair. He called the child, Sope, as his mother did. In her tongue it meant *Only Son*, for he was the only child the strangers had left to her.

    Weakened by grief, she died of fever during the winter. When the storyteller rode away in the spring, he took Sope with him, remembering the Twisted Hair who took him when he was a boy without a mother. The journey was less lonely now. His heart grew lighter as they rode together through the land. When he saw how quickly Sope learned the stories, and how well he understood the wisdom they contained, he was at peace for he knew there would be a storyteller to take his place.

    His spirit was still strong but his body was worn by a life that spanned many generations. Even a man who has been touched by the Nunne'hi must reach the end of his time in the world. He watched as Sope learned well and became a strong young man.

    Harvest time approached when the wind spoke to him. The voice that called was one he had waited many long years to hear again. The Twisted Hair said he was free from his burden and could now leave the lowlands and begin the journey home.

He did not tell Sope this would be their last journey together. "It is time for you to see the place where the wisdom keepers wait. There you will learn many things I cannot teach you," was all he said.

They traveled inland toward the mountains, keeping to the forests and away from places where the strangers lived. On a wide path covered with pine needles, he climbed down from his horse and walked. The path was soft under foot. The scent of cooking fires brought the promise of a feast to come. From far away he thought he heard a child's voice,

"He comes."

At the top of a rise, he stopped and pointed across the valley toward the mound shaped outcropping of stone on the mountainside. "This is where the wisdom keepers live," he said.

When they reached the mound, Sope was eager to hear the songs of the holy people. He purified himself and the storyteller with a smoking sage bundle, then with a reverent heart, climbed to the top of the mound. Quieting his mind, he sat still and silent in a sacred manner, and listened for the story that would be his to take to the people.

He noticed the silence, the absence of birdsong or insects and knew this was a place of the Nunne'hi. The only sound was a distant drum beat, then a song of welcome and blessings drifted through the stone. The song became a story of the world Sope would see as he walked the land alone. The storyteller waited by his side through the day, watching while Sope learned the story that was his to tell. In the evening, Sope still listened to songs of loneliness and duty, but other voices began to sing in the storyteller's ears.

"He comes,"

One voice rose above the others. "Welcome home," it called. His heart danced to the beat of the drums under the mound but he would not join them yet. He waited with Sope, watching him rise to stand tall and proud and begin twisting strands of his hair. The work of the Twisted Hair would continue as long as they were needed in the world.

With the twisting of his hair, Sope took on the mantle of the storyteller and knew it would be a long and lonely journey for he would leave Sha-cona-gee alone. Tears glistened unshed in his eyes at the thought of parting. The storyteller embraced him and said, "Go, my son. Tell the people we are here. When you are old and tired, come to this place to rest."

The time had come to pass the great totem staff on to the next Twisted Hair. Sope's hands trembled when he lifted its weight for the first time. The same Nunne'hi who had bestowed long life on the storyteller so long ago, placed his hand on Sope's head and gave him the gift that allowed him to remain in the mortal world beyond the appointed days of a human being.

The storyteller watched for a moment, but the voice he had waited so long to hear, called from the base of the mound. Twisted Hair waited. He seemed little changed, though many seasons had passed since they parted. The only mark of age was a touch of grey among his twisted ropes of hair.

When they embraced, the years fell away and he looked beyond the grey stone of the mound to see a place long passed from the world. Unchanged faces from generations ago smiled welcome. Old friends ran to meet him while familiar voices called him home.

"He Comes."

He lifted his head and began to sing. He had come, bringing stories of the people.

CHAPTER 4

UNTO THESE HILLS

Strength and long life came with the touch of the Nunne'hi but for Sope, it could not ease the pain of what he knew. The story he had been given to bring his people was too terrible to tell without some thread of hope to soften the pain. When he was alone, he returned to the top of the mound. The future the voices sang was beyond the worst imaginings, but there must be more. Surely there was a way to turn aside the destruction they foretold, and he would not leave the mound until the wisdom keepers imparted it to him. This too, must be a part of his story.

No sound broke the silence and no voice rose through the stone. He called out to the wisdom keepers, but they did not answer. He sat on the cold stone and watched the sun set behind the mountains. The full moon rose and shimmered off the mist, and still he waited alone without food or drink.

On the third night, his vigil tired him so that he fell asleep. Vivid dreams came at once, filled with images of the Ani'yun Wiya dressed in rags and walking in the snow. They looked back at the valleys and mountains formed by the wings of Grandfather Buzzard and wept. The trail ahead was long and marked with shallow graves. They grieved the deaths, but less than the loss of the land that was the very flesh and bones of the ancestors whose spirits lingered to empower holy people to keep the sacred ways and hold harmony in the world. They mourned the loss of secret places where the invisible immortals watched over them and Awi Usdi ran in the forests.

He saw it all taken away.

He watched the Ani'yun-Wiya walk away from the Smoky Mountains and valleys of Sha-cona-gee and cried aloud in his sleep. "Is there no word of hope I can give?"

His vision returned with an image of a man in a long black coat, kneeling on the ground at the head of a great line of the people. Pale strangers stood nearby with their weapons. The man in black lifted his hands toward the sky and began to speak in a loud voice. "I will lift up mine eyes unto these hills from whence comes my help." He said more while the people listened with downcast eyes. Then, one of the strangers shouted a command and fired his thunder weapon. Whips cracked and wagons filled with people lurched forward. Children and elders leaned from them and shed silent tears as they looked back on the home they would never see again.

Among the wagons, a few rode horses, but most walked, bowed down by sadness. A stiff cold wind tore autumn's last brown and gold leaves from ancient trees. Needles of icy rain cut through thin clothing. The people looked back in sorrow for a while, then turned their faces west to the trail ahead. The Ani'yun Wiya were leaving Sha-cona-gee.

At sunrise he woke from his dreams and took up the totem staff of the Twisted Hair. There was no more to learn from the wisdom keepers. Their sorrow was as great as his, but it was his fate to suffer the devastation ahead with his people.

He was no longer young when he walked away. The Nunne'hi's touch could keep his body strong and youthful for generations, but he had witnessed scenes that added ages to his spirit.

In the little village by the creek, he rested for a time. When he told them what he had seen, the elders wept with him. Young men spoke with courage of how they would come together with others of their people and stand against the strangers. No enemy could defeat them if they banded together. In sadness he listened and said nothing. If brave talk could give them hope, it was good.

He encouraged them with stories of other brave men and women who would help keep a remnant of their people alive. Somehow, a few would remain behind to hold their spirit in the land. The voices of the wisdom keepers under the mound had promised, and it would be so. The homeland would not be lost forever. He told them of the man dressed in black. The words he spoke confused them, but they would remember: "I will lift up my eyes unto these hills from whence comes my help."

Before he left the little village by the river, he carried stones to the grave of his mother and built a mound over her bones. His vision had shown him that one day no trace of the town would remain. Perhaps a mound of stone would last and mark the place where he always came when he craved the feel of home. There would be nothing else.

CHAPTER 5
KANAGWA'TI

𝒲here once there was an Ani'yun Wiya village, a house stood alone at the bottom of the hill. Twisted Hair remembered how the people rushed out to greet him when he last stood on this hilltop, but no one welcomed him this time. His people were gone and the strangers lived there now. He turned away and traveled along the ridge back into the forest.

Two women waited among the trees. There was no sign of a trail where they led him, but he followed. He knew no other way to the town where they were headed except the one he had traveled long ago and it was no longer safe. With what he carried in his pack, it was best to avoid meeting other travelers. The gift of the Uku to the children's children must be taken to a place where it wasn't likely to fall into the wrong hands, and given to a man who would know how to use it. Perhaps it would help them hold a place for the people in the sacred land.

The women did not need a path. Through trackless woods and hills, they set a rapid pace. At night, they watched while he slept, then woke him at day break to continue the journey. He was as tireless as they. Though silver threaded through his twisted hair, his body was still young, and stronger than when he last journeyed through these lands.

At the edge of the forest, a river cut through the valley and around green hills. They ventured beyond the cover of a spruce grove to look down at a strange town of rough houses. Men shouted to each other in the muddy streets. Twisted Hair had traveled among the tribes of all the land, learning the tongues of many people but the language of these men was strange to him.

The two women understood and knew this place was not safe. They turned back to the cover of the forest but not before a pale man on horse back rode through the trees and saw them. He whipped his horse into a run and came at them with his weapon drawn. The women urged Twisted Hair to run but he held back. He could not leave them to face the stranger alone. One of them pulled him away, leaving the other to stand alone. He protested, until the woman reminded him of the value of what he carried in his pack and the strength of the woman they left behind. A Nunne'hi woman had nothing to fear from a mortal man. They had not gone far when she caught up with them, unharmed by her encounter.

Another day's journey brought them to their destination. An Ani'yun Wiya village hidden deep in the Smoky Mountains. The two women vanished into the forest and left him to enter alone. There were no welcoming cries. Warriors with lances were the first to meet him and more like them guarded the walls. He was not admitted until he spoke in their tongue and told them his name. In disbelief, the warriors stepped aside, and then followed him into the narrow twisting entry.

A warrior called aloud, "He is come. The one who was promised is here."

When he was inside, the people gathered round him, their eyes alight with reverent awe. They touched his garments and wondered at their richness.

A grandfather reached out to stroke the twisted strands of hair and said, "Another Twisted Hair came here many seasons ago. He had a simple name and told of a hidden town where the old ones wait to speak. He said a great Twisted Hair lived there and would come to us in times of need."

They offered food, but he refused. The smell from the cooking fires tempted him, but he would not eat yet. He had fasted since he left the hidden village in preparation for what he had come to do. He asked to be taken to a man he knew only by name. Kanagwa'ti, he was called. The Water Moccasin.

"He is an outsider," the elder said. "Not one of the Ani'yun Wiya."

"But he is a man of courage and wisdom who honors the ways of our people," Twisted Hair answered.

They offered lodging. He accepted, only to honor their hospitality, for he would have no time to rest. They took him to the house of Kanagwa'ti. The young outsider welcomed him to lodge with him and his Ani'yun Wiya wife.

When they were alone, Kanagwa'ti asked, "Why have you come? We have been told you would return when our peril was greatest. Do you come to warn us? Can you tell us how to fight our enemy?"

Twisted Hair said, "I have come to find the only one who is strong and pure enough to use an ancient power to help our people. With it, he will see that a place is held for us in this land."

Kanagwa'ti asked many questions that only a wise man would ask and though the answers were strange and terrible, he listened. "When you find the one to whom you will entrust this gift of power, I will be at his right hand," he said.

"You are the one I seek," Twisted Hair said. You will be trusted with great power and a terrible burden and you will be alone it its use. If you use it rightly, you can save us. If you are weak, you will be a part of our destruction. You can refuse if you wish, but you must do it now. Once it is in you hands, it will be too late to turn aside."

Kanagwa'ti paled, but did not back away. "How do I prepare?" he asked.

"We will go to a place apart where you will learn the secrets of the Uku. For seven days, you will not take food or drink. After your purification, you will receive the gift he sends you." The Twisted Hair stood and helped Kanagwa'ti to his feet. The sun was setting over the mountains and the people waited.

With the lighting of evening fires, drumbeats called the Ani'yun Wiya together. They circled the fire and waited expectantly. The promised one had come.

He stood before them and raised his hand in greeting, then began to speak. The stories he told were not as wondrous as his presence, for he was a legend come to life and standing before them. At first he told stories they recognized. Late into the night they listened, until one by one the children slept. A few men and women tired and left the fire. Those who remained understood the deepest meaning of the old stories and heard the wisdom within them. In them were answers to many of their questions. They would be remembered and told in generations to come. The old ways were brought to mind and lived again.

Kanagwa'ti spoke little but understood even more than the wisest elder. Twisted Hair saw this and was pleased. He would need to know more than any other for knowledge of the old ways would ease his burden. A holy man sat by Kanagwa'ti's side. He had proven himself to be strong and wise and would be of great help to the outsider. Both he and Kanagwa'ti listened closely to every word when Twisted Hair his next story, and only they understood the truth behind the legend of Uktena and the Ulunsu'ti. The others remembered the story but thought it only myth. Kanagwa'ti looked at the deerskin pouch across Twisted Hair's shoulder and knew it held the great crystal from the serpent's head.

Twisted Hair shifted the pouch as if it weighed too heavy on his back and then sat on the blanket beside Kanagwa'ti and the holy man. He had one more story to tell before he left with the outsider to begin his preparation. The people huddled closer to the fire, gathering nearer to the storyteller. They waited in silence for him to begin his next story for he had said it was one they must remember and pass down through the generations. He drew on the pipe and watched the smoke circle upward then in a quiet voice, he unfolded a mystery.

"In the long ago times, the ancestors of the Ani'yun Wiya walked away from the North lands. They searched for a place of harmony. Here in these mountains called Sha-cona-gee where the smoke of the first people still lingers, they found what they sought.

In the land they left behind, the people knew only war. It is said each man's hand was lifted against his brother and no tribe was friend to any other. The chiefs became thirsty for the blood of their enemies, and all were their enemies. For many generations they battled, and few remembered that human beings were all related and had been given a place on Earth to live together as brothers and sisters. No one spoke out for peace.

When all harmony among created beings had been broken, a great man came to their lands. He walked among the warriors and spoke of a Great Tree of Peace. Beneath it all living beings walked in harmony. Its roots grew deep within the earth and spread through the land, uniting all places. The trunk of the great tree reached the above worlds and its branches spread out to shelter the Earth. Among its leaves dwelt all the created beings.

One of the chiefs had become the most evil of them all. It is said he became so wicked that he devoured his slain enemies. When the Great Teacher of Peace spoke, even he listened. A vision of the Tree of Peace broke the evil in his heart and gave harmony to his spirit. He traveled with the Teacher to other tribes and spoke of peace. The people listened. Warring tribes united into one great nation. Since that day, they have walked in harmony, strong in the teachings of The Great Tree of Peace. In unity they prospered, rejoicing that war had come to an end. As long as they remembered the Teachings of the Great Tree, no man would raise his weapons against another.

Twisted Hair lowered his eyes and looked into the fire, as if he had nothing more to say. The people were confused. A warrior was the first to speak. "Why do you bring teachings of peace when our enemy stands at the gate? Are we to lay down our bows and give them our land?"

Twisted Hair said, "You are to teach your children that all human beings are the children of one creator. Hold the teachings of peace in your heart until a time when this is remembered, but it will not come in your day. The same great teacher told of a great battle that was yet to come. This battle, he said, would not be among the tribes, for their union would hold. The war to come would be fought by two serpents. These were the words of the Great Teacher of Peace.

"A great snake will come from afar and lift his head above the land. A red snake will arise and go to meet him. His welcome will be mocked and the battle between the two serpents will shake the world for many generations. The red snake's strength is great, but in time it will fail while the white snake's power will increase. The day will come when the red snake will be defeated. He will lie as one dead, his spirit gone from him."

He waited while they thought of the strange things he had told them. First, of the teachings of peace, then of war that spanned generations.

Finally, Kanagwa'ti said the first words he had spoken that evening. "The white snake is here. He builds his houses along the river and hunts in our forests. Many are here already and there will be more."

The holy man beside him nodded. "The red snake lay as one dead. Are we the red snake who will die?"

Twisted Hair lowered his head sadly. "The red snake is our people. Like him, our children's children will be as dead people, for their place in the world will be taken away. They will wander in strange lands and be as hollow vessels, empty of spirit. Many will feel shame for their blood. They will forget the tongue of the ancestors and the wisdom it once spoke, and become like the children of the white snake.

Do not despair, for a time will come when the children will look to the sky and see a sign. When they see it, they will know their day of exile is over and the spirit of our people will return. By this sign they will know the time has come. Look to the eagle. When you see her fly her highest in the night and not rest until she alights on the moon, then the red snake will rise, shake off his wounds, and stand proudly over his lands."

Twisted Hair wrapped his robe around his shoulders. Never before had he told this story and it drained his strength. He would leave it with these people. In the faces around the fire he could see the promise that it would be repeated many times. The white snake, the red snake and the eagle would be remembered. This much of his work here was done.

One more thing he must tell them, a thing they would not like to hear, then he had other work to do.

"In generations yet to be, the children of the white snake will come to the red snake's children to learn the teachings of The Great Tree of Peace and the sacred ways of the ancestors. Some will say, "No. They have already taken too much." Do not refuse to teach the children of the strangers. It is through them that the sign of the Eagle will come."

He had told the story he came to tell. Before long, the sun would light the Eastern sky. It was time. He beckoned the holy man and Kanagwa'ti. The holy man would be a comfort to the young outsider and help him bear his burden. They left the others by the fire, still speaking of the things the story-teller had told them. Beside the river they purified themselves with smoke, then seven times immersed under the chilling water. With prayers, smoke and water, they brought harmony to their spirits and made ready.

In a protective circle created by fresh cedar branches and the smoke of their purification, the storyteller opened his pack. The thing he freed from its wrappings lay before them and caught the glow of the first ray of the rising sun, devouring it and leaving a trace of darkness where it had been.

The holy man moved away from it but Kanagwa'ti stood fast. "This is the Ulunsu'ti?" he asked.

Twisted Hair nodded. "From among all our people, you are the Suye'ta, the chosen one. You were chosen as the one who can use the Ulunsu'ti without selfish desires or foolish vengeance, to preserve our people. We will suffer greatly in times to come, but if you use this wisely, our people will not perish."

The Nunne'hi had chosen wisely. Kanagwa'ti nodded assent, and listened to learn what he must do. For seven days, Twisted Hair, Kanagwa'ti and the holy man stayed apart from all others. They took no food or drink and spent their time in prayer, visions and dreams. Kanagwa'ti would need help from the above beings for the work he must do.

On the seventh day, when Twisted Hair had done all that could be done to prepare the outsider, they purified themselves once more and Kanagwa'ti took the deerskin pack and what it held. It was his now, for good or ill. They returned to the village and feasted together, then Twisted Hair took his leave. The young outsider must stand or fall without further help from him for he could stay no longer. The years that had not touched him in the healing village under the mound, pressed down on him here. The Nunne'hi women waited to take him home.

He marveled at the beauty he would leave behind in the world outside. Many years would pass before he saw it again, and it would be changed. Perhaps Kanagwa'ti's village would no longer stand when he returned. Terrible changes would come to the world of the Ani'yun Wiya and he would not be there to offer the comfort of his stories. The boy who had left him to walk the land had traveled long and grown old. Another had taken up the great totem staff and begun the journey. A Twisted Hair would always walk among the Native people of the land to tell the story of their people.

With one last look at the world beyond the village walls, he walked through the rock face of the Council House Mound.

He was home.

CHAPTER 6

SOPE'S JOURNEY

Sope stood beside his mother's grave for awhile and looked back at the little town. It would be a long time before he returned. Perhaps by then it would be gone. The journey he had to make was farther than any he and the storyteller had ever made, but the song of the wisdom keepers had said he must go. Knowing only that his path was toward the west, he mounted the horse the storyteller had given him and left the little town behind.

He lodged that night in a village he had visited many times with the storyteller. When they saw he carried the totem staff, they did not need to ask why. Sope was the new Twisted Hair and they honored him as they had the one before him, but it was in sadness they gathered to hear the story of how it came to be. He told of the journey to the hidden town and of the Twisted Hair who waited there to welcome the storyteller home. To tell it gave him comfort, for it reminded him they would both be waiting there for him when he was old and tired.

There was more he must tell and only one night for the telling. By sunrise, he must be on his way west. He began by speaking of the spirits of the grandmothers and grandfathers whose memories were held in the land. "Where their bones lie, their flesh has become the land. Their breath is the air we breathe and their voices speak in the wind. They nourish us in the fruits of the earth. This land is the gift of the Great One to our people. The sky people look down upon us here and the Nunne'hi live among us. Never forsake them, for when they are forgotten, our people will be no more."

He was silent for a time to let them think of what he had said. Perhaps they thought he spoke of such things because of his grief for the storyteller but his sadness was far greater than they knew. Soon they would understand. He watched their faces when he told of his visions and saw his own fear reflected in their eyes.

When the young men objected, saying no one could take the homeland from them, he said, "In my journeys I have seen the great mound cities of the lowlands lying abandoned. The people who built them have disappeared. Their tongues are forgotten and their stories are no longer told. Their lands are claimed by the strangers. In the mountains formed by the wings of Grandfather Buzzard, the Ani'yun-Wiya still live, but the strangers even now build houses on our lands. They name us Cherokee, perhaps because they try to call us by the name of our home, Sha-cona-gee. They are different from the ones who took so many lives in the lowlands and along the water, for they seem to come in peace. They trade with our people and call us friend. In this is great danger. Our warriors have no need to fear our enemies, but with kind words and promises, we will be broken."

While they talked of these things, he left them and went to the house of the chief and slept. It was not yet light when he awoke. The chief and some of the elders waited outside his door, bringing his pack filled with provisions for a long journey. He had thought to slip away unnoticed, but it was not to be. They walked with him for awhile, talking of the things he had told them. Before parting, they asked him the same question he had asked the wisdom keepers. "Is there no word of hope you can give?"

He gave them the answer he had been given. "The sprit of our people is in Sha-cona-gee. Here, the wisdom of the ancestors will live. As long as a remnant of the Ani'yun-Wiya remains among these mountains, the sacred ways that give us our strength will not be forgotten. Teach this to your children. Tell them they must not forsake the homeland of the ancestors. Here lies the hope of our people."

His journey led him beyond the hills and into the low country. He entered villages where they waited for the return of the one whom the storyteller had promised long ago. Some of them had traveled to the mound in Sha-cona-gee to seek wisdom from the wisdom keepers. The knowledge they brought home sustained them through times of trouble. Sope listened to their stories and then told his own. He spoke of the hunger the strangers had for the land, not out of love or honor of the Earth as the home of the ancestor's spirits, but as a thing to possess. Then, he told of the journey he must make, and the reason he traveled west.

"The Great One has given visions to men of other tribes, showing the coming of strangers whom they called, *The Turtle People,* and the changes they bring to the land. They have seen the future and speak of things to come in the days of the children's children. I go to learn their stories, and bring them to the wisdom keepers. Knowledge can be held safely there, even when it is forgotten in the world beyond the sacred mound. Though we are scattered and driven from our homes, there it will be remembered that we are all one in wisdom, spirit and blood. As long as this is known, and a few of us remain on the land, we will live."

He departed that village at day break, as he would many others, to continue a long hard journey. In time, he left all that was familiar far behind, and rode through flat dry lands. Everywhere he went, they remembered the Twisted Hair and welcomed Sope to lodge in their homes. Even to these strange lands, a few of the strangers had found their way. He traveled many days with a great tribe that moved their whole town to the banks of a great river. There, they caught fish and dried them on racks in the sun. Among them was a man with red hair. The man had taken a wife from the tribe and she had born him children. Their skin was almost a pale as his and there was a tinge of red in their dark hair. The red haired man had learned to speak the tongue of the tribe as well as others with whom he traded. Sope lodged with him for a summer, listening while he spoke of the ways of his people and learning to speak the language of the strangers. When the tribe left the river, Sope continued his journey toward the setting sun.

Years passed while he traveled. By the time he reached his destination, he had learned many things. He would hold them in his heart, keeping each morsel to enrich the store of knowledge in the hidden village under the mound. He had heard of the journey the storyteller made his youth, but his travels had taken him to the North. All he learned from the people of those lands, he took back to the wisdom keepers. In the dark times to come, they would hold it safely, there where the sacred ways were remembered.

The fullness of his manhood had come to him

by the time he reached his destination. His visions had shown him the place he must go, but even so, he stood a distance away looking at it in wonder. He could see people high up on the walls and hear the voices of the children at play. Houses the same color as the red-brown earth, were stacked one atop another with ladders to reach the upper lodges. Smoke rose from cooking fires and women ground corn in the courtyards. The storyteller had told him what the sacred village under the mound was like when it was still in the world. This town was much as it had been, for this too, was a holy place for the keepers of wisdom.

He walked toward the town, thinking he was unnoticed until a cry went up from the walls.

"He comes."

The people of the town ran to meet him with shouts of welcome. The weariness of the journey fell away and he was at peace.

The people listened with rapt attention while he told of the sacred mound in the mountains, and the wise ones who lived in the hidden village beneath it. He told of the strangers who had come to live among them, and of their greed for the land.

When the moon was high in the sky, an elder man stood and walked away, beckoning him to follow. Other men rose with him and they fell into step with the elder, leaving the people to talk of what they had heard. They wound among walls and courtyards until they reached a circle of stacked stones. Within the circle, a doorway led down into darkness. A hand on his shoulder guided him to the place he was to sit. He had learned many new ways in his journeys and stored them in his heart. They would be taken back to Sha-cona-gee and added to the knowledge of the wisdom keepers. This was another story he must tell when he returned.

From the darkness beyond the closed circle, a light approached and then a torch appeared through an opening. It barely lit the face of the man who set it into a niche in the wall where it cast a dim glow around the underground circle. Someone lit cleansing herbs, and the fragrant smoke swirled among the men. A drum sounded and the elder chanted prayers, then all was silent.

When he spoke again, his voice seemed to come from all directions. "From times of old, we have heard that the three shakings of Earth would be foretold by the coming of men who wore shells like the turtle. When the strangers first came, we knew they were the *Turtle People*, for they walked like men but wore shells that turned away our arrows. This was the first thunder of the shaking of the world."

He fell silent as if to gather his thoughts. A young man handed him a bowl and he drank from it and then began. "I will tell you of things to come, but first it is good to speak of the time of beginnings. In that time, all human beings lived together on an Island in the middle of the great water, for all Earth was one land and all human beings were one people. There was no unhappiness for all pleasing things were there for them to enjoy. For a long time, all the human beings were in harmony and lived in peace as brothers and sisters. War was not known.

A day came when some of the people separated from the rest. They went to live in the Northern reaches of the Island. Soon, another group moved apart to the South of the Island. The ones who where left, quarreled about who was at fault for their leaving, and soon they separated to the East and West of the Island.

As generations passed, they stayed apart until the people of the four corners of Island had changed and adapted to the ways of the places they lived. When each looked at what they had become they said, "This is the way all human beings should be." They looked at the others and hated them for their differences. All harmony among the human family was broken and they began to make war with each other.

When The Great One saw how they fought among themselves, his voice rolled like thunder through the land. The Island shook as he spoke of their pride and conceit, reminding them he had created them as one family of human beings. The battle raged even as the land trembled at the sound of his voice.

For many days, thunder rolled and the Island shook. It did not end until the people talked of peace and ceased fighting. When they promised to walk the path of harmony, the thunder stilled and the Island stopped shaking. The first shaking of the land ended and human beings still lived.

For a long time, the human beings remembered the shaking of their land and walked in harmony. They talked of the thunder and remembered they were all children of the Great One. Their battles ceased, and they were at peace.

In the days of their children's children, the elders who remembered the first shaking had left the world. The story of the thunder that shook the Island was no longer told. Anger grew among the people and harmony was broken. Once again, the people from the four corners of the island gathered their weapons, each crying out against his brother.

Again, a great thunder rolled through the land as the Great One called out a warning. Mountains crumbled and rivers left their beds, and still the thunder shook the Island. The people cried out in fear but as long as brother spilled the blood of brother, the shaking did not cease.

After many seasons, they remembered the teachings of the elders and the sacred way of harmony, and put aside their weapons. The thunder ended and the second shaking of the Island came to an end. For a time, the people walked in harmony and lived in peace as one family of human beings.

There were a few who could not enter harmony nor think of peace. The sickness of their anger spread, and before the generation of the second shaking had passed from the world, they sent young men to make new weapons and prepared for a battle to come.

Now, it is said by the wise, that the Great One will warn once, and the Great One will warn twice, but the third time you stand alone. This is how it happened on the Island of the first people. When the Great One called out to them for the third time, the thunder of his voice caused a shaking that tore the island apart. The lands of the four doors separated. The great Island was no more and all the human beings fell into the sea.

The Great One spared the human beings, lifting them from the water and placing them on the scattered lands. The people from the North of the Island, he placed at the Northern door of the Earth. He named this the White Door, and gave its people two gifts. The first was a stone on which was written sacred words of wisdom and prophecies of things to come. They took the stone and hid it beneath a mountain. In time, they forgot it was there. Some told the stories written on the stone, but did not remember their meaning.

The second gift to the people of the Northern door was the guardianship of fire. He said, "learn all it can teach and the good it can do. When you come together again with other human beings, live in peace as brothers and sisters and bring to them the teachings of the fire."

The elder drank from the bowl and closed his eyes in thought. When he opened them again, he looked at Sope and said, "In speaking of the coming of the Turtle People, you speak of the spreading of the fire, for the nature of the fire is the nature of its guardian. The fire spreads and consumes, but as it spreads it brings together the family of human beings. The Great One wants us to live together in peace as brothers and sisters. The people of the white door keep the guardianship given them by the Great One when they bring us together, but it will be many seasons before we learn to live in peace."

Sope nodded. "The strangers are the people of the white door. Their fire nature causes them to spread throughout the world. In this, they bring the human family together, but many are consumed?"

The elder knew Sope understood. He continued his story. "The people of the Southern part of the Island now lived at the Southern door of the Earth. The Great One named this the black door, and gave its people two gifts. The first was a stone on which was written sacred words of wisdom and prophecies of things to come.

The people of the black door took the stone and buried it at the foot of a mountain, but some remember the writings to this day. The wisdom of the stone is sung in their songs and spoken in their stories.

Then, the Great One gave the people of the Southern door the guardianship of water. He commanded them to them learn its teachings and power and said, "When you come together again with all the human beings, come in peace to live as brothers and sisters and bring to them the teachings of the water."

The people of the Southern door made their first home beside a great river. Its' rising and falling was the rhythm of their life. They learned to live on the richness it brought to their new land.

The Great One placed the people from the Eastern part of the Island at the Eastern door of the world. The Great One named it The Yellow Door, and gave its people two gifts. The first was a stone on which was written sacred words of wisdom and prophecies of things to come. They took the stone to a high mountain, but they did not hide it away. They built a great lodge for it, and wise people still go there to learn of its wisdom.

Then he gave to the people of the Yellow Door the guardianship of the air. He said, "Learn from it. Find what it teaches you, and when you come together with all the other human beings, come in peace to live as brothers and sisters, and bring the teachings of the air." We have been told in visions and dreams that when we see them again, they will teach us to breath in the wisdom of the above beings.

Now, the people from Western part of the Island lived at the Western door of the world. The

Great One named it the red door, and gave its people two gifts. The first was a sacred stone on which was written sacred words of wisdom and prophecies of things to come. The people of the red door took the stone and have kept it safe. The Great One placed it here, in our care. It is from this stone that we learned some of the prophecies of things that are to be.

To us, the Great One gave the guardianship of the Earth. He said, "Learn from her. Find her gifts and when you come together with the other human beings, come in peace to live as brothers and sisters, and bring to them the gifts of the Earth.

When the strangers came to this land, the people of the red door met them bearing the gifts of the Earth, the three sisters, corn, squash, and beans. We have kept our guardianship. Now the human beings have come together again but not in peace. We have not heeded the warnings of the Great One. If we do not learn to live in peace and close the circle of the four doors, then will come the shaking of the earth."

Sope asked, "How will we know when the shaking of the earth begins?"

The elder approached the center of the circle and called for a torch. He uncovered a great stone that lay in a hollow of the floor and held the torch above it. The torch lit up symbols and pictures. Sope looked at it and could almost hear it speaking, so powerful were the images engraved on its surface.

"This is the stone on which is written words of wisdom and knowledge of what is to be," the elder said. "We are the keepers of the stone. It foretells many strange things that will come before the first shaking of the Earth. The coming of the Turtle People is written here, and the changes they bring to our people and to the world. Here you can see through the eyes of one whose vision took him high above the land. When he looked down, he saw what seemed to be many little bugs traveling upon black ribbons across the land. In time, he saw that the little bug would leave the land and fly into the sky. Look for the sign of little bug traveling the black ribbon across the land for it will bring people from he four directions to see each other face to face

The time will come when the little bug takes to the sky. When you see this come to pass, listen for the thunder for it will be the voice of the Great One, calling to our children's children to live in peace. If they do not close the circle of the four doors, uniting the human family, then the whole world will tremble. This is the first shaking of the Earth."

Sope had many questions. When the elder had answered all he asked, he stored the strange story in his heart to take to the wisdom keepers under the sacred mound. He must tell them of a little bug, and of the black ribbon winding across the land. The elder said the little bug would increase until there were more than could be counted, all traveling the black ribbon, before taking to the sky.

When he returned to the hidden village, the wisdom keepers would understand the meaning of this new story. They would keep the knowledge of the signs that heralded the three shakings of the Earth. When it was time for all the people to learn of the little bug which would be the omen of the first shaking, they would send this story to them.

The elder continued with more that he must remember. "If the people do not heed his warning, the thunder of The Great One's voice will roll across the land. Until harmony is restored and human beings walk in peace, the world will shake. If the circle of the four doors is closed, the first shaking will end and the human family will be blessed with gifts beyond our understanding. As long as we live in peace, we will receive all good things.

If harmony is broken and we fall into ways of anger, the thunder will sound once more and the second shaking will come. Tell the children's children to cry out for harmony among human beings when this day comes, for if they do not unite, they will cast the great gourd of ashes upon the land. Where it lands, all life will end like grass in a hot fire. Its poison will spread upon the world, causing great numbers to sicken and die."

Visions of devastation swam before Sope's eyes, mingling with images he had seen atop the sacred mound.

The elder's voice echoed through the circle. "If the second shaking ends before the world breaks apart, you will see many strange things. Human beings will build a house that shines in the sun as if it is made of mica. It will rise high above a great city in the East, higher than the tallest tree. In this house of Mica, the people will come from many lands to talk of peace. For peace to come, all the four sacred colors of the human family must be heard, and the circle of the four doors of the world must be closed.

In the time of our children's children, we must knock upon the door of the house of Mica and ask to be heard, for the people of the Red Door will be the last to speak. We must talk before all the people and tell of the wisdom found on the stone of knowledge. If we are heard, the circle of the four doors will close and human beings will have more time to learn peace.

Tell the children that when they see the nations come to the House of Mica, they must knock the first time. If they are turned away, they must knock again. Four times, they must knock.

Watch for a time when people of many lands will work together to build a house and cast it into the sky. People from all their nations will rise up to live in it. Our children must knock the fourth time before this comes to pass. If they are not admitted before human beings live in the house in the sky, the first thunder of the third shaking will be heard."

In the darkness, Sope's voice sounded small in his ears. "What are the signs of the third shaking?"

The elder continued. "We do not understand the visions, for they show a strange world. We see men who have learned the secrets of life. They make new living things and say it is good. In the time of their children, it will cause great sorrow. They will bring forth animals that have neither mother nor father. Old sickness will come back and new sickness will take many lives. They will use the secrets of the plan of life and change plants and animals until they no longer are part of the harmony of the earth and give no nurture. The Earth will grow tired and fail to bear fruit or grain. There will be hunger. Men will sit beside the river and have no water, for it is not good to drink. A great web will spread around the world, and unite all human beings. If we have not learned to live in peace by then, the first thunder of the third shaking will sound.

Sope trembled at the thought of such a world. It was not a world he wanted to see. To hear it described brought fear to his heart, but this was a story the wisdom keepers must hear. He asked, "What is the sign of the first thunder?"

The elder answered, "It will be heard in a great city with houses so tall they block out the sun. In the morning, the tall houses will stand. Before the day ends, there will be nothing left of them but smoke rising from ashes. When you see this, time will be short for it is the last warning. If we do not listen, the thunders will sound. It is said that a man will look into the sky, and see the stars in the wrong place. Cold lands will become warm and warm lands will be cold. Water will cover dry places and cease to fall in wet lands. In the end, the world will shatter. As in the days of the first people, the land will break apart and human beings will be separated to the four doors of the world again. The great web will be broken."

Sope asked, "If our children's children heed the wisdom of the stone and close the circle of the four doors, what will be?"

"If human beings walk in harmony and learn to live in peace, as one family, they will help the Earth to bloom again. The four sacred colors will be one, and the children's children will be a golden people."

For a time, there was silence while they thought on these things, then the elder spoke to Sope. "Take these words to the hidden village where they will never be forgotten. On your journey, speak of them to the elders of all the people who give you shelter, and tell them to remember. When it is time, we must speak of these things o all the people of this land, even the children of the ones who now bring great sorrow to us, for they too are a part of the harmony. If we are to close the circle of the four doors, they must listen."

The elder gave Sope time to think of what he had heard and store the words in his heart. Then he asked him to speak of his own visions he had seen atop the sacred mound. This would be added to the store of knowledge kept in the dark underground circle. Sope rose to his feet. He spoke of the sacred mountains covered with smoke, and of the sorrow of his people who lived there. When he told of the future he had foreseen, they grieved with him.

Through the night they talked of the things that were to come, and the words of wisdom written on the stone. Sope told them many things he had learned on his journeys, and they were added to the knowledge held by the keepers of the stone.

Outside, the sun rose and traveled across the sky, but its light did not touch the place of mystery where they gathered. Nothing entered that could distract them from their purpose. Wisdom and knowledge were exchanged and understanding began. There was purpose in all things, and it would come with the uniting of the human family and the closing of the circle of the four doors of the world.

When they emerged from the circle beneath the Earth, the moon was in the sky. The elders took Sope apart to purify with water and smoke. He ate well and slept soundly that night. When he arose, his pack was filled with supplies and new clothing. The elder and some of the others came to bid him farewell.

Sope had one more thing to say in parting. "Look to the sign of the eagle, for the time will come when our people will be as dead men walking upon the land. They will breathe and speak, but the spirit will be gone from them. For many years they will forget who they are and the wisdom they hold, but when the Eagle flies her highest in the night and does not land until she reaches the moon, we will live once more." Saying this, he turned his face toward the sunrise and began the long journey home.

CHAPTER 8

GOING HOME

Sope's heart longed to return to the little village by the creek. His dreams told him it no longer existed, but hope refused to die. His journey did not take him directly home but led him to wander among the people. He hunted bison with the plains tribes then listened to their stories of strangers who slew the great beast and left them to decay. He watched the strangers build armed forts on grounds where the bones of ancestors lay. Warriors fought bravely, but for every one of the strangers who died, ten came to take his place.

Sope had no skill as a warrior and could not aid in their battles but he lifted their spirits with promises of a place under a mountain far away, where the wisdom keepers guarded the knowledge that gave strength to the Native People of the land. He had a new story to tell, of the great stone of knowledge and prophesy that waited in a sacred place where holy people kept it safe.

Late at night, when only the elders lingered by the fire, he spoke of things to come and bade them remember. Many years he wandered through plains, mountains, deserts and valleys, always telling his stories and grieving for the people as he saw the changes that came to their lands. When he stood beside the last great river that stood between him and journey's end, his urgency to go home became stronger. The people who made their home on the river banks pleaded with him to stay, for the way was not safe for an old man who traveled alone. When he could not be persuaded, they ferried him across in a boat made from a burned out tree trunk, and watched him walk away.

He stopped on the way to speak with scattered bands of his people, but his stay was always brief. He slept little, telling his stories late into the night, then leaving at the first light of dawn. He must go to Sha-cona-gee, but not until he had walked once more along the banks of the creek where the little village stood.

He arrived late in the evening, hoping to rest in the lodges of his own people. Only scattered ruins remained of the village beside the creek. He found the mound of stone on the hill, covered with moss and shaded by an oak that had grown tall in the years since he went away. It sheltered him that night as he slept beside his mother's grave.

At first light of day, he walked into the creek to spear a fish. On the bank, a child stood watching. His hair was long and dark and his skin a light copper hue. The boy could have been one of the people, except that his eyes were pale green. Sope offered to share his fish with the boy. They sat together, the old storyteller and the child whose blood was of the Ani'yun Wiya, but mixed with that of the strangers. The boy asked many questions, then listened, hungry for knowledge of his mother's people. His father did not allow her to speak of such things in the house he had built for his Cherokee wife and son.

In spite of the urgency to return to Sha-cona-gee, Sope stayed a few more days with the boy. When he left, he knew he would return, for the blood of his people still lived in a few of the people who now made their homes in scattered farms along the creek.

His spirits lifted when the foothills of the Smoky Mountains came into sight. Traveling in the high country and keeping to the cover of the forest slowed his journey but he knew the strangers were more numerous than his own people. He had learned it was best to keep out of their sight.

On a cool autumn day he arrived at a hill that looked down on a house where he thought the strangers lived. It was built in the style of their homes and surrounded by a low wooden fence. A man and woman stooped over rows of potatoes they unearthed and tossed into baskets. As if sensing his approach they stood and looked toward the hill then raised their arms in welcome and called to him in his own tongue. They were Ani'yun Wiya. Leaving the baskets in the garden, they welcomed him into their home.

It was good to be with his own again, to eat the food he remembered and listen to familiar words. They told him about the changes that had come to their home land.

"The strangers take our houses for their own," the woman said. "At first they shared our land, but soon more of them came. They forced us off the places they wanted to live and crowded us out of our homes. Now, they build their towns on the land of our ancestors."

Sope remembered his vision long ago as he sat atop the mound. He had hoped it would not come to pass while he was still in the world, but it had already started.

As soon as they knew he had come, Cherokee people traveled from communities all around. They gathered in the farmhouse and waited for him to speak. Word of his journeys had spread among all the

Native people of the land. Perhaps he could offer wisdom that would turn aside the flood of strangers that threatened to force them from their homes.

He listened to their fears, but could do nothing to comfort them. His words were more warning than solace when he said, "your hope lies here in these hills. This is your strength. The spirits of our ancestors speak to us here and teach us to remember. Even when our people are scattered afar, they will look to this land for knowledge of their blood, and they will know, this is their home."

He rested for a few days, but when the others traveled to sit in council, he went with them. He listened while they talked of the trouble that had come to the land. Some of those who spoke looked and dressed much like the strangers. They talked of courage, but fear rang in their words. Warriors wanted to defend the people the way warriors have always done. Others could see that Native People were hopelessly outnumbered. Elders, like the wise Junaluska advised that some of the ways of the strangers were good and the people would do well to learn them.

They talked of a man called Sequoyah who showed them how to put Cherokee words on the talking leaves like the strangers did. They showed him a stack of them and called it a book. With Sequoyah's writing, the Cherokee could speak to each other with strange marks on the leaves. There would be a newspaper too, like the strangers had. Even now, they prepared for it in a town they called New Echota.

A few did not see any cause for fear. They lived side by side with the strangers, and prospered. Cherokee warriors fought with them in battles, and some had married the strangers. Their children had the blood of both. "The white men have become our brothers," they said.

Others said, "With kind words and promises, we will be broken."

Sope listened, but memories of his vision atop the mound ran through his mind.

A man rose to speak. "Andrew Jackson is the new president," he said. "He will not betray us. Do you not remember that our great war chief, Gul ka laski, who is now called Junaluska, fought at his side in the battle of horseshoe bend. When a Creek warrior would have slain the white soldier, our chief shot the Creek and saved his life. The president is brother in battle to our own warriors, and owes his life to Junaluska.. He will see that out lands are protected."

There was truth in those words. They could trust the man who had come to plead with Junaluska to bring his warriors to fight at his side. He had said that the American's would have lost that battle without the help of Gul ka Laski and his Cherokee warriors. Had he not made a vow of friendship and promised to reward them.

They left the council and returned to their homes. Sope could see that the Cherokees were outnumbered in their own homeland. Their well tended farms were the envy of many of the strangers who resented the fact that people they considered savages, lived better than they. The Cherokee owned the best land to be had, and those who begrudged it would stop at nothing to take it. His vision on the mound was always before his eyes now. It wouldn't be long. He could do nothing but walk among them and learn their story. It unfolded as he watched.

The cry of "gold" rang out in the North Georgia Mountains and sealed the doom of the Cherokee way of life. Perhaps they would have been allowed to remain on their farms, but lust for gold was even greater than greed for land. With subterfuge and deception, unscrupulous men gained title to the sacred homeland. The Cherokee were ordered to leave.

Junaluska and Chief Drowning Bear went to Washington to plead with President Andrew Jackson. Had they not fought beside him in the battle of Horseshoe Bend? Had not the war chief of the Cherokee saved Jackson's life when his enemy would have brought him down? The president was a brother in battle, and would never dishonor himself by deserting a brother warrior, especially one to whom he owed his life.

In disbelief and with broken hearts, they returned to their people. Jackson had turned his back on the Cherokee. They were betrayed. They had trusted the leader of the white people. Drowning Bear's own son had died fighting beside Jackson at Horseshoe Bend. Many other warriors had died fighting Andrew Jackson's battles, but now, he did not need them. He had no help to give when the Cherokee fought for their home.

The next part of the story was almost too painful to observe but Sope knew he must. The children's children would need to know. When the column of soldiers rode onto Cherokee land, he remembered the face of the man who led them. He had seen it in his vision long ago, before the man was even born. Now, he knew the name of the man who had troubled his dreams many nights. This was no dream. General Winfield Scott was flesh and blood and riding into the homeland with many soldiers. He sent his men to round up the people at the point of rifles. There was no mercy for man woman or child. Even the dead were not respected. The soldiers came to a gathering in a small cabin where a mother and father prepared their dead child for burial. The family never knew what happened to the child's body for they were forced to leave him there.

A woman, dragged from her bed, was too sick and weak to go on. When she died on the road, her children were made to leave her there on the ground and walk away. In every mountain, valley and cove the soldiers searched out Cherokee people and drove them off to stockades built to hold them until they could all be marched to the west.

A few fled to hide in the mountains. If they stayed in their homes the soldiers would take them to be imprisoned in the stockade. Hiding out in caves or makeshift shelters, they lived off the land. If enough of them could remain in the homeland to continue the fight for the rights of the Cherokee to live on their own ancestral homes, maybe their people could return one day. From a distance, they watched as squatters moved into their houses and harvested their crops.

Sope's vision had not shown him one whose story he would tell. The man's name was Tsali, and his courage would give hope to generations yet to come. Without him, perhaps all those who remained behind, and all hope for the return to their homeland, would have been lost.

When the soldiers came for Tsali's family, as they had for many others, they had no choice but to go with them to the stockade. On the way, some of the soldiers assaulted Tsali's wife. Tsali, his brothers and sons defended her. A soldier was killed.

There would be no mercy from General Scott for Indians who had taken the life of one of his soldiers. The only hope for Tsali and his family was to flee to the hills.

General Winfield Scott could not allow them to go free. To do so might encourage other Cherokees to revolt. Scott sent out soldiers with orders to bring Tsali, his brothers and sons back to the fort where they would be put to death.

The soldiers searched without success, for Tsali knew the mountains of his homeland far better than they. General Scott's solution was cruel but effective. He announced to all who could hear that if Tsali and his family surrendered, all the other Cherokees hiding in the hills would be left alone. If not, Scott's soldiers would hunt down the last man, woman or child until there was not a single Cherokee left in their ancestral land.

The one who took the message to Tsali was a white man, Will Thomas, known to the Cherokee as Will Usdi, Cherokee for 'Little Will.' He was given that name when Chief Drowning Bear adopted him to take the place of his son who died in the battle of Horseshoe Bend. Will Thomas had proven to be a true friend to his adopted people and one of the few white people who could still be trusted in those troubled times.

Chances are, Tsali would never have been found. He, his brothers and sons could have stayed where they were and saved their own lives at the expense of their people. Instead, they returned to the General's headquarters with Will Thomas, knowing they faced certain death. It was the only way to save the people who would remain behind and preserve a place for the Cherokee in their homeland.

Tsali, his brothers and his sons were condemned, and taken to a field to die before a firing squad. The soldiers raised their rifles and waited for the order to fire. A man dressed in a long black coat stood nearby with his wife. They were white, a missionary couple who had stood by the Cherokee in their troubles. Suddenly, the woman dashed in front of the soldiers with their rifles. Clutching Tsali's youngest son to her breast, she ran until she was out of sight. He was little more than a baby and she could not bear to see him face the rifles. Her husband stayed to offer comfort to those who would die, reading from his book that promised they would live again in the above world.

Sope turned his head away when the shots rang out. The man in the black coat said prayers for the dead, then left to find his wife and the Cherokee child. Tsali's son would be safe.

A young soldier found Sope standing alone, watching them walk away. The soldier spoke to him in the Cherokee tongue. "You must come with me, grandfather." There was a hint of regret in his voice. Sope walked with him to the stockade where he was imprisoned with the rest of his people. He sat on the packed soil just inside the gate with no shelter from sun or rain. The young soldier gave him a blanket and a drink of water from his canteen. A child came and leaned against the soldier's leg. "He is kind to us," she said to Sope.

If there was kindness among the soldiers, it was a story Sope wanted to remember. He asked the soldier how he had come to be among Winfield

Scott's men. The young man told him the story of how he became a friend to the Cherokee. His name was John Burnett, he said. He was hunting one day when he was young, and came across a Cherokee boy who had been shot by a band of hunters. The boy escaped and hid out under a rock shelf. When John found him he was almost dead from thirst and loss of blood. He cared for the boy till he was able to travel, then took him home to his people. He stayed with the boy's family and learned to speak their language. He later joined the American Army and went away, but he remembered the family of his Cherokee friend and tried to make the way easier for them and their people. Since he could speak their tongue, General Scott brought him on this campaign as an interpreter.

  Sope watched, and noticed that Private Burnett was not the only soldier who did what they could to ease the suffering of the Cherokee. Their kindness was all that kept some of the weakest alive in the heat of summer.

  The season passed and cold came early that year. A chill October morning came when no kindness could ease the anguish of the Cherokee. Drizzling rain slanted in a freezing wind, cutting through thin clothing. A long line of wagons stood ready to roll, loaded with the weak and old. From the back of his aging horse, Sope watched the vision he had seen so long ago, become reality. Some rode horse back. Most would walk the long trail. The soldiers lined up with their rifles.

  He saw the man in the long black coat climb on a loaded supply wagon so he could be seen and heard by the people. He bowed his head and prayed, then lifted his eyes to the encircling mountains and called in a voice that all could hear, "I will lift up mine eyes unto the hills from whence cometh my help." He read those words from his holy book, but when the people looked to the hills, they thought of the ones who were hiding there, waiting for the day when they could reclaim the land of their ancestors. When the soldiers shouted orders to march, they said farewell to the beloved land they would not see again, and turned their faces to the west.

Men who thought of the land only as a possession could not imagine the depth of sorrow its loss brought to people for whom it was a sacred homeland where the ancestors lay and memories stretched back through generations of Ani'yun-Wiya.

The long hard winter set in and added to their misery. Wind driven sleet and snow took their toll. Many had no blankets. Most had only the ragged clothes they wore when the soldiers drove them from they homes. At night they slept in the wagons or on the cold ground. Every daybreak found more dead from exposure.

Chief Ross's wife gave up her blanket to a sick child. She died during the night and was buried beside the trail. There was no coffin for her body, not even a blanket to wrap her, for they were all needed to warm the living. She would have had it no other way.

Through the coldest months of the winter, they walked the Trail of Tears. Four thousand graves remained to mark their passage.

Gul ka Laski chose to walk the trail with his people. He had taken the name, Junaluska. In the tongue of the strangers, it meant, *'He Tried But Failed.'* President Andrew Jackson would have allowed him to stay behind at his farm on the banks of

Deep Creek, but his place was with the Cherokee who needed him most. Perhaps his leadership would make the way a little easier.

He suffered with them until they reached the lands in the West, where they would be allowed to make a home. When he could do no more for them, he turned his steps back to the Smoky Mountains. Any further help for his people would come from the hills of home. If the spirit of the Cherokee was to survive, they must hold a place in the homeland of Sha-cona-gee. The few that remained behind, hiding out in caves or whatever shelter they could find would need him.

Sope joined the little band that traveled home with the great chief, watching and remembering. They arrived to find that Will Thomas was already doing his part. As a white man, he was allowed to buy land and hold title in his name. The impoverished Cherokees worked hard and gave all they could spare to purchase land they had once owned.

Their work, along with the others who had hidden out in the hills, restored a place where the descendants of the Ani'yun Wiya could hold a place in the land of the ancestors.

In the years that followed, Sope told their story to the children. They must remember the heroes of their people. Tsali and his brothers and sons. Junaluska, the Chief who led the people to the West and then walked back to fight for the land. White people like Will Thomas, the man in the long black coat, and his wife who saved Tsali's son from the firing squad, and all the other who's courage spared Cherokee lives. He told them around many evening fires. The heroes of the people must be remembered.

In the days when the people had lost their spirit and walked as dead men on the earth, great deeds such as theirs' would lift heavy hearts.

The heroes grew old and left the world. Junaluska's bones rested on a hilltop near a town of the white people. He had seen the realization of his hope to regain a home for the Cherokee in the ancestral lands, and helped it be declared a reservation that could not be taken from them again.

Sope had stayed long enough. The rest of the story of the Eastern Band of Cherokee would be for someone else to tell. Early on a spring morning, he stopped atop the hill long enough to place seven small stones on Junaluska's grave to honor the great man. Filling his eyes and heart with the beauty of the greening mountains, he prayed for his people, then took up the totem staff and set out toward the place where a mound of stone stood atop his mother's grave. He lived there beside the grave, waiting. The small boy, who had shared a fish with him was an old man now, but he had a grandson who listened to his father's stories and watched for the Twisted Hair to return.

The boy found Sope on the creek banks and asked for a story. Sope began that day to teach him for there were many things the boy must learn in the short time Sope had left in the world. In days to come, the people would need a Twisted Hair and he had little time to prepare the one to whom he would pass the totem staff.

He had already heard faint voices in the wind.

CHAPTER 9

OF THINGS TO COME

It was a small gathering that night around the fire. Most of the people who had come to dance and remember in the sacred circle, had gone home or wandered in the field beyond the dancers. The few who were left, talked about the old times when their people were the only ones who lived in the Smoky Mountains they had called Sha-cona-gee. They repeated ancient stories of sacred beings whom the elders claimed lived among them; The immortal Nunne'hi, the tiny Yunwi Tsunsdi, the little white deer they called Awi Usdi, and all the others who were seldom, if ever, seen anymore. Some said they no longer existed. Many believed they never had, except in stories told by the grandparents.

The world had changed since the days when their ancestors were called Ani'yun Wiya. Some of the changes made them fear for the land. The waters flowed in the rivers and creeks as it always had, but they couldn't drink it. Where fish once filled the streams, few were seen. The smoky mist that shrouded the sacred Mountains now poisoned the trees and caused sickness for children and elders. If ever they needed the wisdom of the sacred beings from the old stories, it was now.

A young woman had started to speak, saying she would soon leave the Smoky Mountains and go to live far away. She spoke to honor the memory of her grandmother whose bones rested on the hillside that rose beyond the field. The few around the fire settled down to listen, but the voice of a new arrival broke the silence.

The man who walked into the circle was not known to them, but he was welcomed. He greeted them in the language of their people, and then sat quietly, warming himself by the fire for an early spring chill touched the mountain air. They watched him, wondering who the strange man could be.

He was one of their own people, this they could see. They marveled at the intricate beading and quill work in his deerskin leggings and tunic. His moccasins were fine enough to be the envy of the best dressed dancer, but they bore the marks of wear.

One of the young dancers stared in open admiration of the stranger's garb. He had gone to great effort to assemble regalia as close to the traditions as possible, but when he saw the man's clothing he knew he had fallen far short of his goal. He sat with the elders and waited for the man to speak.

The man said nothing while others returned to the circle or gathered nearby in the field, wondering about the visitor who had appeared from nowhere. They could see he was a full-blood. His features, his bearing, and his fine copper skin attested to this fact, but his hair was worn in a way that only one elder among them had seen. She was a grandmother, older than anyone could remember. Her stories of a wandering old man who remembered for the people, were mostly ignored by the young, but now, they wondered if she knew more than she had said. It was the visitor's hair that made them think of her tales. She had described it as a mark of a holy man of old. Long to the waist, she had said, and twisted into ropes and held at the crown with beaded thongs.

This could not be the same man, for he seemed young. While he wore his hair as she had described, it was black as night. Only a thin streak of white shot through the strands to mark the passage of time. His face was unlined and his body straight and strong.

He reached into the deerskin pouch at his side and withdrew something. The growing crowd strained to see what he held. It looked like an ordinary newspaper. He sat as if reading it by the firelight.

The man that sat nearest him asked if he was with the group from the Cherokee Nation out West, come to attend the pow-wow. He shook his head and told them he lived a few miles away in Graham County, and then looked at the young woman who was speaking when he arrived. "Is that not your home too, uweji agehya?" He used an old term meaning 'my daughter.

She nodded, but said nothing. Her family had lived on the Cheoah in Graham County for generations and she had never seen this man. This was a puzzle for in such a small community, no Cherokee went unnoticed.

The man spoke to her again, asking her forgiveness for the interruption. "I would be honored if you would allow me to listen while you speak of your grandmother." He sat on a blanket an elder man offered to share, and listened.

The young woman stammered at first, a little intimidated by the stranger, but the story she told was a gift from her grandmother and she told it in her memory.

"I live in a little house beside the Cheoah River. Soon I will go away to live with my husband in a town where I can't hear the River's song. Only my grandmother understood how this would sadden me. Before she walked over to the other world, she gave me a story of another girl who loved River as I do. This is the way my grandmother told it to me:

Long time ago in a village beside the river, a baby girl was born on the coldest, darkest night of the coldest, darkest winter. The first thing the little baby heard was the wind howling outside. The cold found her, even wrapped in a warm blanket and held close by her mother.

Darkness filled the lodge she had entered and it seemed to the baby girl that the whole world was dark and cold. She cried in fear. Outside, River heard her cry. He sorrowed for her, knowing she had never seen the sun and didn't know of summer. River sang to the baby girl. His song promised sunshine, flowers and bright colored birds who would sing their own songs. He sang of how warm she would feel in the spring and how soft breezes would take the place of the howling wind.

His song eased her fear and she understood that the winter would go away and warmth would come. The smile she sent River warmed him and cracked the heavy ice that rode his back.

Through the winter, River sang to the baby girl every day. Soon she could sing back to him, in her own way, and her smiles and laughter warmed him.

At last, Cold Maker went away and Sun warmed the village. The mother laid her baby on the soft grass of River's bank, and she heard his song. When her mother looked away, the baby crawled as fast as she could to the very edge of the water. In her joy at seeing the one who had sung away her fear, she reached out to touch him and fell into the rushing water. Her mother cried out for help. Her father and the other people of the village hurried to rescue her but she was nowhere to be seen. Young men took canoes out to search but could not find her.

When they had given up hope and sat weeping beside the water, a spray from the rapids lifted the child and laid her upon the shore. Her people knew they need not fear the river. The baby girl was safe in his care.

When she was older, her father cut a tree and made a canoe just big enough for a little girl. In it, she traveled with River and he told her stories of all his journeys. She wanted to go with him to the place where he joined the great water, past the forest and green fields, to see all the things he told her about in his songs. He said no. She must stay close to her people.

Her people called her River Girl for that is where she could always be found, in her little canoe on the river. When she was a young woman, many young men came to ask her mother for her as a wife. The mother said, " She will have no husband but River."

A time came when the rains did not fall. Game was scarce in the forest and the fields yielded little. In the village beside the river, the people worked hard to store enough to last for the coming winter. Cold Maker came early and stayed long.

The River Girl's people had enemies who did not provide for their own, but sent warriors to take that which others had prepared. They attacked her village before the sun rose, bursting from the forest without warning to steal the grain and meat they had stored.

The people fought bravely. When River Girl's father fell, she took up his bow and fought in his place. When her people saw her courage, they were inspired to fight even more bravely. The enemy was defeated and the winter provisions saved.

There were many dead warriors that day. The river girl and her father were among them.

Now, there is a place where only fallen warriors can go. The spirit ponies always come to gather the warrior spirits and take them there. River Girl's father and the other dead were mounted and ready to go, but she too was a warrior and had earned a place with the fallen. They searched for her but she could not be found. Not in the forest or village or near her mother where some spirits might go.

At last, when there was nowhere else to look, her father heard her voice. It was faint, almost drowned by the deeper voice of River, but he heard it clear. She sang along with River, for in death she had joined him to journey to the places he sang about. Her voice can still be heard, singing with him, and will for as long as the river runs."

The young woman sat beside her mother, who embraced her and brushed tears from her cheeks. It is hard to send a child into the world. In the old days, a husband would have come to live with the mother's clan, but times had changed.

The stranger stood and thanked her for her story for it was one he had not heard before. "I too am a storyteller but most of my stories are far older than the one your grandmother gave you. Some you still know, and others you have forgotten." He lifted his voice until even those still strolling about in the field beyond the circle heard. "I have come tonight to bring a story that is even now unfolding."

From the darkness around the ceremonial grounds, people hurried back to listen. The elder woman who had spoken of him whispered, "The Twisted Hair." The words carried as if shouted into the silence. The stranger stood tall and still, waiting for the right time.

In the expectant silence, the old woman rose to her feet. Her eyes filled with tears and she hesitated to speak, but the stranger nodded in her direction. She spoke haltingly at first, and then in awed tones raised her voice to tell an almost forgotten story. In her words, the hidden town under the sacred mound lived again. She brought to memory the elders who held the wisdom beneath the mound. Then she spoke of the Twisted Hairs of old who had walked the land.

A young man asked, "What has this to do with the stranger?"

With shining eyes, she looked at the man. "In the days of the arrival of the Turtle People, the Nunne'hi took a healing village into the mountain under Counsel House Mound. There, the wisdom keepers hold the knowledge of the ancestors. The great Twisted Hair left the world to go into the hidden village. When he is most needed, it is said he will come to us with word from the keepers of wisdom within the holy place."

The man thanked the old woman for remembering and then waited while the crowd grew. When they were silent and expectant, he began to speak. His voice was soft, but it carried far beyond the fire.

"Listen closely, for I will not come again while you are in the world. It is for you to remember my

words, and see that they are made known to all, for they are the stories or our people. As long as they are told, we will live. The story I bring you tonight is known by only a few, but it must be told to many, for within it is the secret that must be made known if human beings are to remain in this world. I have returned to tell you of things yet to come. Long ago I came to this place. The museum was not here then, or highways and buildings. There was only a village where a man named Kanagwa'ti lived. In that day I brought a story of the Great Teacher of Peace, who came to the North lands many generations ago when only our people lived on this continent. In that day, he told of a time when a great white serpent would come.
  A great red snake would go out to meet him. The two serpents would begin a battle that would go on for many seasons. The white snake would gain size, strength and power. The red snake would become smaller and weaker. In time, only the white snake would stand. The red snake would lie upon the ground, his spirit gone from him. His people would wander lifeless in the land, as if they were dead but still walked.

     You have heard this story many times, and you know who the two serpents are. For many generations, our people have walked this land as if there was no spirit in them. Some were ashamed of their blood and became more like the strangers than their own people. Many of the sacred ways of the ancestors have been abandoned and the land where their bones lie, are torn by the machines of the white snake's children.

     Long ago, I stood in the place where we now stand, and spoke to the Ani'yun-Wiya who lived here.

I gave them the words of the great teacher of peace who told of the two serpents, and of the promise of the day when the life spirit would return to their descendants. I spoke of a sign that would mark the return of life and hope to our people. The sign was not for their day, but for their children's children. The promise was for you.

You have heard it said, "Look to the Eagle, for you will see her fly her highest in the night, and she will not stop until she sits on the moon. When this sign is seen, it will mark the return of life to the people of our blood. When the Eagle has landed, the red snake will arise.

You have seen the sign of the Eagle. On the night you heard the words, "Tranquility base here, The Eagle has landed," that prophecy was fulfilled. The Eagle flew her highest in the night and sat upon the moon. That is when the spirit of life came to rest once again in the hearts of our people. It is time to come alive and claim your place in the land. Take up the guardianship given to you by the Great One, for you are the keepers of the Earth.

The prophecies tell of great harm that will come upon the world, and it has already begun. I have been away from you for a long time, but others like me have traveled the land, holding wisdom in the mortal world. One who walked among you for many years will soon finish his journey and come home. His sadness has been great, for his eyes have witnessed the falling away of our people. He has walked among people who showed him no honor, and only the children heard his story. It has been his joy to see the Eagle land on the moon, and watch the awakening of life in our people. In clothing, hair and speech, you show pride in a heritage that some of our people have forgotten. Where once the laws of the strangers forbade you to hold festivals and honor the above beings as our ancestors did, you remember the old ways.

    The awakening has begun, and you are ready to hear prophecies that are given to you and your children, for I have come to prepare you for the time to come. Before we speak of things that are yet to be, it is the way of our people to recall the time of the beginning."

    The people listened while he brought to their memory the story of the first human beings and the three shakings of their Island world. He spoke of how all the people of the broken Island were scattered to the four doors of the world. He reminded them of the great stone of wisdom and prophecy, and of the guardianship given to the people of the four doors.

    "The people of the Northern door were given the guardianship of fire. Their fire nature has caused them to spread and consume. In this, they serve the guardianship and bring together the family of human beings. In the work of their hands, they honor the fire. In all their works, you can see the fire, and it serves to bring human beings from the four doors of the world to know each other again as they did in the beginning when all people lived together.

    We are told we must learn to live as one human family, and close the circle of the four doors, or the shaking of the world will begin. The Great One has spoken many warnings and given dreams and visions to mark the approach of the time of purification, and now all the human family must hear his words. There are stories that have been told many times, but only within our own circles. Now it is time to tell them openly to any who will listen, for if the world is to stand, all must hear."

The circle around the fire was now filled. People stood in the field beyond, listening, and all heard clearly. No sound broke the silence. Even the children listened in silence.

"In the beginning, the world was shaken apart by three great wars. When the first people could not come together as brothers and sisters in one family of human beings, the world on which they lived was torn apart. Their story is kept in our memory as a warning, for we must do what they could not. As the Great One designed, we are all to live as one people.

Two times the Earth has shaken. Twice, we have heard the thunder and heeded the warning, but it is said that the third time, we stand alone. On the third shaking, only human beings can prevent the world from shaking apart. If harmony among the human family is not restored, you will tear apart the world, and Earth will be purified of the wrongs of man.

Long before the first shaking, you were warned by those who saw visions and dreams. You have heard of the vision of the little bug that traveled the land on a black ribbon. Human beings moved about the land because of the little bug. This was the first warning from the Great One. When the little bug flew from the black ribbon and took to the sky, the wise ones knew the people of the four doors of the world must come together and speak of peace. But the circle of the four doors was not closed. The people of the four sacred colors of the human family did not meet to talk of peace. The first shaking of the world began.

You have seen the little bug. Even now it travels on a ribbon of highway and has brought you to this place. When it took to the sky, the wrath of the Great One sounded throughout the four doors of the world. The Earth shook. Death and sorrow filled all the land as had not been since the beginning.

In the time of the first shaking, the elders warned that the circle of the four doors must be closed, that all the human beings of the earth must come together and talk of peace or the second shaking would come. This would bring even greater harm for the great gourd of ashes would be cast from the little bug in the sky and fall upon the earth. Where it fell, people would wither and die like blades of grass in the fire. Poison from the great gourd of ashes would spread afar, causing all in its path to sicken and die. The great evil it brought to the Earth would never be rubbed out.

You have seen the first shaking of the world, and still the circle is not closed. You have seen the second shaking. The gourd of ashes has fallen and still the circle of the four doors has not closed. The four sacred colors of the human family have not joined as one family.

The keepers of wisdom watched as the warning of the first shaking was forgotten. The second shaking has come and gone and still, there is hatred among the family of human beings. They spoke of the warriors in the sky who dropped the gourd of ashes upon the land. The nation who dropped it must be warned, for in the third shaking, it will fall upon its makers.

Visions showed other signs of the approach of the third shaking. A House of Mica was seen, built in a great city in the east. It rose higher than the tallest tree and gleamed in the sun as if made of mica. It those days, the one who saw it did not know of glass. He saw that representatives from all the people of the four doors were to come together in that great house and talk of peace. If this came to pass before the last sign, harmony would be restored and humans would live as brothers and sisters as the Great One wanted. If it didn't take place, then the third and final shaking would come and Earth would purify herself.

    When the United Nations Building rose above the tallest trees, with walls of glass gleaming in the sun, the elders heard it was a place for all people to talk of peace. They said, "Ahh, the House of Mica." They watched as people from the Northern door, the Eastern door, and the Southern door came to sit in council together and talk of peace. But your people of the Western door were not among them. The circle of the four doors was not closed.

    They talked of this, and of the prophecies that said they must knock four times on the door of the House of Mica and ask to speak. If at the time of the last sign, and after the forth knocking, the people of the red door were still outside the circle, the third shaking would come.

    It is well known among you that a delegation, assembled from different tribes and Nations of the Native people of this land, traveled to The House of Mica and knocked upon the door. They said. "We represent the indigenous people of this continent and we ask to be heard." They were turned away and went back to their homes. The circle of the four doors was not closed when they knocked the first time.

    Wise men and women of our blood talked of this, and of the signs of things to come. The prophecies spoke of a time when human beings would learn the plan of life and create new living things. They would change animals that already lived into something different than Creator made them. They would say, "This is good," and would release these new living beings upon the earth. Some would warn against these beings, but their creators would say, "They do good and not harm." In the time of their children's children, these creatures will bring great trouble.

Other visions showed a time when the water would be poison and cause the fish to die. Clean water to drink would be scarce. The life would go out of the soil, leaving it weak and unable to produce enough food. Trees would begin to die when they were young, and from the tops down, not from the roots up as is nature's way for an old tree. It was said that seeds and plants would be changed until they no longer brought forth grain and fruit, or that the fruit and grain they bore could not be eaten. Even the three sisters, corn, beans and squash would fail to nourish. New sicknesses would come and bring death. Old sickness would return with greater power.

Strange things were foretold that caused wonder even to the holy people. It was said that a great web would spread around the world and unite human beings from the four corners of the Earth. We have watched as the telegraph, then the telephone came, and now the web is here, and human beings are connected.

Keepers of wisdom watched as one after another the visions have come to pass. We knew when delegates from the red door knocked upon the door of the house of Mica and asked to speak. Three times they knocked, and three times they were turned away. The last sign before the third shaking was at hand. They must knock the fourth time for if it appeared before the circle was closed, the purification would begin and none could stop it.

Long ago, a dreamer saw a time when human beings would build a house and cast it into the sky. People from all the lands would rise up and live in the house in the sky. This was the final omen, for if the people of the red door were not welcomed in to the house of mica when the house in the sky was completed, the beginning of sorrows would come.

It was foretold that we would look into the sky and see the stars in a different place, as if they had shifted from their path to the other side of the world. Lands that were once cold would be warm and warm places would see cold and ice. Many animals would leave the world for there would be no place for them. The balance between the animals and human beings would be disturbed and the natural order would be no more. Visions showed a great city. There were houses, so tall that when you stood among them you could not see the sky. At sunrise, they were there, but by midday, there would be nothing left but smoke rising from barren ground.

The wisest among you have seen many of these signs come to pass, and know their meaning. You have spoken of how all the people of the four doors must come together in the House of Mica and talk of peace. You have watched the people of the white door, the yellow door and black door find a place in the council circle, but the people of the red door have not. Three times they knocked and three times they were turned away.

When your people heard that a space station would soon be in the sky, and people of many lands would live there, the elders knew, they must knock again for the fourth and last time. This time, refusal meant it would be time to warn the people to go to the high mountains where perhaps a few would survive."

He opened the newspaper he held folded in his hand and gave it to the old woman who had called him Twisted Hair. The woman opened it and read the date, December, 1996, the year that had just ended. On the first page she saw pictures of people she recognized. Native people, speaking before the leaders of all the nations of the world. She passed the paper around, so they could see once again a story that had given them great pride, as the Twisted Hair repeated the story from memory.

"On November 22, and 23, 1993, delegations from the Algonquin, Lakota, Hopi, Iroquois, Mikmaq, Huichol, and Mayan Nations, spoke before the United Nations and delivered messages handed down through the generations of our people. They spoke of prophecies that warned of what is to come if we do not listen. Their message was: "We must stand together, the four sacred colors of man, as the one family that we are, in the interest of peace. We must raise up leaders of peace and unite the religions of the world as a spiritual force strong enough to prevail in peace."

The newspaper passed from the circle, on to the crowd that had gathered in the field. Twisted Hair raised his voice so all could hear. "It is for you to remember what has been foretold. You live in the shadow of the third shaking of the world. The guardianship of Earth is given you, and her fate is in your hands. Your young will see changes you cannot understand, for if the world stands, it will be made new. Human Beings will change. The four sacred colors will unite, and a race of golden people will come into the world. Great truths will fall and greater ones arise, but you must remember. The one truth lives within the stories you hold in your heart. All wisdom is hidden within, and the wise will find it. Keep them always, for they are your hope."

A man from the North held the newspaper up and read of how representatives of the Iroquois Nation had met in New York's Central Park. There they held a ceremonial planting of a symbolic Tree of Peace. He spoke of the Great Teacher of Peace who had come to his people long ago and told its story. "Yes, there is hope in the stories of our ancestors," he said.

Twisted Hair listened for a while, long enough to know they understood. No one noticed as he walked away from the circle. Two Nunne'hi women waited to guide him home. He followed, for he did not wish to linger in the strange land he had once loved. The shape of the mountains had not changed, but an unfamiliar smell hung in the air.

A few stars shown dimly in the sky, but far fewer than he remembered. He listened for the voices of night birds but all he heard was the dull roar of the little bugs as they traveled the ribbon of highway.

In great sorrow he followed the two Nunne'hi women back to the hidden city under the mound. Sha-cona-gee was no longer home.

CHAPTER 10

OLD SOPE

*J*ust to the North of the city of Atlanta Georgia, a creek flows past a bend where a little village once stood. Beside its banks, a mound of stone protects the bones of a woman who died of grief long ago. Now, the creek winds past big houses and highways. Golfers at the Atlanta Country Club can hear it rushing by on quiet mornings. It flows past the ruins of an old paper mill and beneath the wooden covered bridge at Concord, and beyond. They call it Sope Creek, and say it is named for an old Indian man who came to wander its banks, back before the Country Club or the covered bridge or the paper mill were built. A few scattered farms stood along the creek then, after the Indians who used to live there were gone. Children who grew up on those farms said an old man came and told them stories. They said he was very old, with long white hair worn twisted into ropes and bound with strips of leather. His clothing was strange, made of leather and beads, but worn and old.

The parents never saw the old man, but they listened when their children told his stories. They must have believed in him, because they gave the creek the name the children called him. Sope Creek, they called it, and it is still known by that name.

People who live along the creek have heard of him, and wonder who he was. Some think he must have been a ghost, for surely there were no Indians around in those days. They had all had been taken away.

The children believed he was real. He told them stories of how he traveled along the creek long ago, before there were farm houses, when there were still Indians around and their villages stood along its banks. They spoke of how he came to the villages in the old days to tell his stories. When his people were gone, marched away to the west, or to a shallow grave along the trail, he stayed behind and told his stories to the children who came to live in on their land. He was safe with them,

No one has seen Old Sope for a long time now. He doesn't come to the children who play at the creek anymore. He is gone. He left them one day and began a journey toward the Smoky Mountains.

Tired and lonely, he trudges a no longer familiar trail. He will not return. His journey is done.

Down a cool path still carpeted with pine needles, he walks, his eyes on the mound of stone that stands out from the mountain on the other side of the valley.

Does he hear a faint cry?

"He comes."

Smoke from cooking fires waft through the breeze. It gives him strength, for he has not eaten since his last journey began.

The cry is louder, "He Comes!

He can see them, two men waiting at the foot of the mound. One so familiar, his heart aches with the joy of reunion. Another, more legend than man, stands beside him. Their voices rise above the rest. He begins to run. With each step, he grows stronger.

Years of loneliness slip away. He hears the sound of dancing water and remembers when creeks still ran clear, the mountains were green and cool and storytellers were met with joy as they drew near. The cries have become a song.

"He comes."

The stone mound shimmers and fades from sight. Green hills rise beyond the river. Sweet odors greet him and voices call his name. The storyteller embraces him and Twisted Hair welcomes him inside. His journey is over. He is home.

Twisted Hair brings the stories of his people.

GLOSSARY

<u>Ani Waya</u>- Wolf People. People of the Wolf Clan, one of the seven clans of the Cherokee, or the Wolves themselves. Believed to be the guard dogs and hunters of Kenati, the first man.

<u>Asi</u>- The sweat lodge. Often used as winter sleeping quarters in cold weather. It was a low circular structure of logs covered with earth. The fire smoldering within it kept it warm.

<u>Awi Usdi</u>- The mythic chief of the deer tribe. He is described as snow white, about the size of a medium dog, with a large rack of antlers. He has always been friendly and helpful to humans but his first duty is to his own people, the deer. He allows hunters to take a reasonable number of deer, if the appropriate ceremonies are kept, and punishes with sickness, any who kill more than they need or forget the rituals.

<u>Dakwa</u>- A mythic great fish. In modern usage it is the name of the whale.

<u>Galun-lati</u>- Above or on high. The Cherokee overworld. The first home of the Cherokee. Many of the mythic beings have returned there and no longer live on the earth. Some, like Awi Usdi visit earth to care for their people here. The Uktena now lives there for he is too dangerous for the earth. Since death is of a very temporary nature there, little harm is done even if he does kill someone. The Cherokee version of heaven.

Ghigham- A title sometimes used for the *Beloved Women*, who were women with a great deal of authority in Cherokee society. They were known by other titles, such as *War Women,* or *Pretty Women.* In old times they often earned the title in battle. A recent Beloved Woman was Maggie Wachacha, a Snowbird Cherokee who served as a council scribe and translated proceedings into the Cherokee syllabary for many years. A joint council of the Eastern Band and the Cherokee Nation designated her and Lula Gloyn of the Qualla boundary, as Beloved Women in 1984. They earned the title based on long years of service to their people, a reputation for wisdom and gentleness, and their role in maintaining the history, knowledge and traditions of the people.

Raven Mocker- Ka'lanu-Ahyeli'ski. A kind of witch in Cherokee mythology. They were shape changers who could take on the form of a large raven and fly through the air. You could tell them from real ravens by their size and the fact that fire sparks would come from their wings as they flew. They were among the most feared of the witches because they could become invisible, enter the home of a sick, wounded, or old person, and take their heart without leaving a scar or any sign. The victim would die, and as soon as the raven mocker ate the heart, he would have the life which was left to the victim. In this way they lived many years more than mortals, and could live indefinitely as long as hearts were available.

Nunne'hi- [nun-ya'-hee] An invisible race of Cherokee. They were full sized people, very handsome and richly dressed. They usually lived in places where others wouldn't chose to live, such as bald mountains, or old mounds.
Cherokee people who have told stories of having been lost and rescued by the Nunne'hi, tell of being taken to their homes which were beautiful with rich fertile corn fields, and well fed and entertained. When taken outside the village and directed to the path home, they looked back and could see no sign of the Nunne'hi town. Some say that time was different in the Nunne'hi villages and what seemed like a single day there could be weeks, months or even years in the real world. There are numerous stories of Nunne'hi warriors intervening to assist the Cherokee in battle.

Tsali- A Cherokee hero. Revered by his people for sacrificing his life and the lives of his sons to save the remnants of the people who were hiding out in the hills to avoid removal to the west. An historical marker honoring him is at the Swain county courthouse in Bryson City North Carolina, for it is on that spot that Tsali and his sons were executed by firing squad.

Uktena- A mythical monstrous serpent who in the in old days lived in the Smoky Mountains. He was large enough to coil around a mountain with his head resting on the crest. He had an enormous appetite and often fed on humans. There was great power in his scales and to own even one gave a holy person or conjuror magical abilities, especially prophecy. At the top of the Uktena's head was the great talismanic crystal, Ulunsu ti. The Uktena had to be slain to obtain it but it was the most powerful talisman known.

<u>Unehlanuhi</u>- Creator. Also the name the Cherokee call the Sun.